GABE'S SECRET

by
Amy Durham

Gabe's Secret
Copyright © 2016 Amy Durham
Published By Amy Durham
ISBN: 978-0-9974958-0-5
Print Edition

Editor: Taylor K's Editing Service
Cover Artist: Tracy Stewart (www.simplybookish.com)
Formatter: BB eBooks (www.bbebooksthailand.com)
Proofreaders: Dawn Laurent Bourgeois, Glenda Edwards,
and Teresa Reasor
Contact Information: amybdurham@gmail.com

OTHER BOOKS BY AMY DURHAM

Once Again (Sky Cove #1)
For Once: A Sky Cove Short Story (Sky Cove #2)
Once And For All (Sky Cove #3)

Dusk

Asher's Mark (Resolution Book #1)

ÐEÐICATION

To Glenda

Friendship is always a treasure… and yours is the best one of all. I don't think I could live without the laughs, the sisterhood, and the trust that exists between us. You are such a gift in my life.

Oh… and thank you for making me read my first romance novel!

ACKNOWLEDGEMENTS

Writing may seem like a solitary venture, and in many ways it is. However, it takes much more than just me and a lot of quiet time with my computer to pull off the writing and publication of a book. I'd like to take a moment to thank the people who were a part of bringing Gabe and Rachelle's story to completion.

Dawn, Glenda, and Teresa – Thank you for your willingness to proofread and catch all my typos and missing commas!

Dustin Quillen – Thank you for helping me figure out how to describe Gabe's tattoo as a work of art, not just a two-dimensional bunch of ink on his skin.

Taylor Kent – Thank you for your tremendous editing skills.

Paul Salvette and team at BB eBooks – Thank you for making the interior of my books look so professional and appealing.

Tracy Stewart – Thank you for creating a beautiful cover that truly brings Gabe and Rachelle to life.

Kevin, Kelly, Eli, & Reece – Thank you for the craziness and love you bring to my life. And thank you for being proud of me. I love you all.

Kentucky Independent Writers – You are a fantastic group of people, and I am so fortunate to know you all. Thank you for the friendship and camaraderie we share.

Chapter 1

GABE

HER LONG CASCADE of black hair sends my heart rate skyrocketing. I should be used to it by now. Her presence does it to me every time.

Friday nights at Ugly Mug are always kind of crazy. Even though there's no live music tonight, the local college kids who are still on summer break pack the place. Especially the ones who are too young to legally drink. But even in the sea of people swarming the inside of the coffee shop, I spot Rachelle Taya's petite frame as soon as she walks in. No surprise. I've been zeroing in on her for the past several months. She just doesn't seem to notice.

Or maybe she's just immune to my mad flirting skills.

Grace Ballard is running the register, and from my spot in the kitchen, I watch as she takes Rachelle's order. As the manager, I normally don't work the kitchen, but since we're slammed tonight, I'm helping out. Her order placed, Rachelle makes her way away from the register, and despite the crowd, finds a vacant table on the opposite wall. Once seated, her face drops into her hands and she rubs at her temples. Even from across the room I feel the stress radiating from her.

I slip out of the kitchen and take the ticket from Grace's hand before she can clip it on the order holder.

"I'll take care of this one," I say.

Grace narrows her eyes but says nothing. I'm certain she's noticed I give Rachelle special attention.

From the shelf full of random mugs, I grab the one with giant lip prints. Yeah, it's kind of pathetic. I want to kiss Rachelle so bad I'm using a freaking coffee mug as a substitute.

Glancing at the ticket, I'm not surprised. Rachelle often orders the same drink. Medium roast coffee with cream and a shot of hazelnut flavor. After filling the mug, I place the orange cranberry scone on a saucer and head through the crowd to the corner table she's occupying. Staring out the window, she seems a million miles away.

"Service with a smile," I say, sliding the coffee and scone in front of her and dropping into the seat across the tiny table from her.

Rachelle shakes her head and laughs. "Why do you always give me the VIP treatment?"

I answer without missing a beat. "Because you're hot."

"Gabe!" she scolds me, but it's only half-hearted. Her eyes meet mine for a split second – the silver and diamond of her nose piercing sparkling in the light – then she picks up her coffee and takes a drink. Something's on her mind. In the past couple of months, I've become fairly good at reading her body language, and busying herself with her drink is her go-to when she's got shit on her mind and wants to deflect attention away from herself.

She hasn't yet figured out that she has my full attention whether she likes it or not.

"Hey, it's true," I say with a shrug, keeping it light for the moment. "There's also the fact that I know your boss and the guys you work with, and I take good care of my friends."

"You're a good guy, Gabe." Her admission nearly knocks me on my ass. All this time I thought she'd pegged me as some kind of superficial playboy. "The way you had Asher's back, and Grace a job. You kept an eye on her until he pulled his head out of his rear end and made things right with her."

"Grace is a great employee," I answer honestly. "It's a win-win for everybody."

She nods, sipping her coffee and hiding behind her mug. The silver stud below her bottom lip – I forget what that piercing is called – clinks against the mug. I smile and decide it's time she knows I'm tuned in to her mood.

"Something bothering you, Rach?"

Her eyes shoot to mine. "Why do you ask that?"

"You're here alone," I say, leaning my elbows on the table and bringing my face closer to hers. "You were looking out the window at nothing when I walked over, and you're hiding behind your coffee mug."

"Wow." She sits the mug down on the table. "You're observant. I guess that comes with working in a place like this."

I shake my head, leaning closer still. "Comes with having a major crush on you."

She makes a *tsking* sound, dismissing my admission as sarcastic flirting. I've let her get away with that before.

Not this time.

"I wasn't joking, Rach."

"Gabe." Her voice is nothing but a whisper and her eyes drop to the table, refusing to meet mine.

Her hands are wrapped around the mug, and with a gentle ease that I always feel toward her, I reach across and pull them away, enfolding them both in my grasp, enjoying the warmth that remains on her skin.

"If you haven't noticed, I've been trying to get your attention for the past few months."

She's quiet for so long I'm afraid she's not going to respond. When she doesn't pull her hands from mine, I take it as a good sign.

"I thought you were just kidding around," she finally says, lifting her eyes to look at me.

I shake my head, my heart hammering hard against my chest. It's never mattered this much before whether or not a girl returned my feelings, but at this particular moment, I feel like my life depends on it.

Her gaze softens, and one corner of her mouths lifts.

It's a small smile, just a hint of one actually, but it's there, and I grab hold of it with everything in me.

I don't want her to feel pressured to respond verbally, so I return to my original question, giving her hands a final squeeze before letting go. "What's wrong, Rachelle? And can I help at all?"

"Family issues," she sighs. "Nothing you can do except bring me coffee and a scone."

"I can relate to family shit," I say. And yeah… if she had any idea.

"It's complicated," she goes on. "And, it doesn't necessarily involve me directly, except that my mom's going to need some help in the next few weeks."

I glance up at the clock above the cash register. "Tell you what, hang around another forty-five minutes or so until closing. We can hang out and talk in private… about whatever you want. We'll chill for a while, and you can pretend like whatever's going on doesn't exist."

"I don't know, Gabe." She's skeptical, and I hate it.

"Rachelle," I say, taking her hand again. "Just hanging out. Nothing else."

She smiles, full on this time, and nods her head.

I barely manage to keep from leaping to my feet and pumping my fist in victory.

Chapter 2

RACHELLE

GABE LOCKS THE door and flips the sign to *closed* as the last of Ugly Mug's Friday night crowd heads out. I'm still in my seat in the corner of the room, and I watch as Gabe walks to the counter to give some final bit of instruction to Grace and the others as they work to close up shop.

I'm still kind of stunned by Gabe's admission that all his flirting has been legitimate. I'm almost embarrassed by the number of times I rebuffed him, thinking he was just being his normal, goofy self. And now that I've agreed to spend the last hours of the evening with him, something inside me simmers with anticipation.

When Gabe turns toward me and smiles, my breath catches and my heart does a weird somersault-type roll.

"Come upstairs?" he asks when he reaches the table.

Okay, I hadn't been expecting that.

"Upstairs?"

The shock must show on my face because Gabe quickly adds, "I live in the apartment upstairs. It's quiet."

The look of genuine compassion and kindness that

spreads across his face catches me off guard. His bright blue eyes hold nothing but kindness. I'm used to happy-go-lucky Gabe, who thrives on light-hearted silliness and seems to have no cares in the world. As he holds his hand out to me, silly Gabe merges with sweet Gabe and there's no way I can keep from reaching out to him. Warmth spreads through me as his hand envelops mine. Awareness simmers along my skin, as if my body is waking up to the fact that Gabe Jenkins has a thing for me. My pulse flutters in my throat as I try in vain to take in enough oxygen. Hand in hand, we walk past the counter where Grace is wiping down the surface. She gives me a warm, knowing smile, and I smile back, even though butterflies have taken flight in my stomach.

Cutting through the kitchen, Gabe pulls a key from his pocket and unlocks a door that leads into a tiny cube of a room. A door leading to the back parking lot is on my left, and to my right is a flight of stairs that I assume leads up to his apartment.

Gabe moves to the first step then turns back and offers me his hand once again. Somewhere inside I know that he's offering me more than just help up the stairs. He's asking for my trust and affection. And even though the thought of it seems strange and overwhelming, there's no way I can stop my hand from reaching out for his. When his fingers clasp securely around mine, a smile lights his face and our eyes lock. Without words, we ascend the stairs toward his apartment.

The stairway is narrow, so I stay a step below him the

entire way up. The well-worn red shirt he's wearing stops at the waistband of his jeans. From this angle it's difficult not to notice the way they hang low on his hips and hug his thighs.

I'm not sure what I'd expected, but when Gabe pushes the door open and flips the light on, I'm surprised – in a pleasant sort of way – at the simple neatness of his place. It's basically a studio-type floor plan, although it's not nearly as cramped as some of the studio apartments I looked at several years ago. To the right of the door we just entered is the kitchen, with one long counter and set of cabinets along the wall and an island surrounded by four barstools. Directly in front of us is the living area. Naturally, a flat screen TV hangs on the exposed brick wall, and an oversized brown leather couch is positioned in front of it.

Like most guys, Gabe doesn't have a ton of personal or decorative stuff in his apartment. However, I can't help but smile when I notice that the curtains on the living room window are a collage of vintage album covers, and the surface of the giant coffee table in front of the sofa is painted like a Union Jack flag.

"Typical bachelor pad," he says, tossing his keys on the bar. "But, at least I'm not a slob."

"I never thought you would be," I admit. "You run a tight ship downstairs, so it figures you'd be pretty organized in your personal life, too."

"You've already had coffee, but can I get you something else to drink?" he asks walking to the kitchen and pulling open the refrigerator. "Root beer, bottled water, and apple juice are your choices."

"Water is fine," I answer, glancing in the fridge and noting the absence of beer. Strange for a guy Gabe's age, but I don't mention it.

Toward the front of the room, a partial wall extends halfway across the width of the area. I assume his bedroom is beyond it, hidden from the rest of the studio space.

"Bedroom is kind of a loose term," he says, noticing where my gaze has wandered. Stepping beside me, he offers me the open water bottle. "It's more of a sleeping area, but it works."

"I guess if you're living by yourself it's not that big of a deal," I respond.

He shrugs. "If it's got a bed and some pillows, it's all I need." Gesturing to a door just beyond the kitchen counter, he continues. "Bathroom and laundry are in there."

"Efficient, but still roomy," I say, nodding to the open floor plan that flows from entryway to kitchen to living area. "I like it."

"Are you going to tell me what's got you down in the dumps?"

Leave it to Gabe to jump right to the point. I hadn't planned on unloading my family drama on him, but just now, standing in his tidy, very cool apartment, something in me wants to open up.

So, instead of locking it all inside like I'd normally

do, I plop down on Gabe's couch and start talking.

"My mom's run into some financial trouble," I begin, staring down at the bottle of water in my hands. The cool of the bottle contrasts with the warmth I feel in Gabe's presence.

Beside me, the couch dips as he sits right next to me rather than at the other end of the couch. "It's weird because she's always been okay with money. We never had much, but once she figured out how to budget, the bills always got paid and we always had food on the table."

"So what's changed?" he asks. "Did she lose her job?"

"I'm not sure what's going on." I notice the way his jeans are wrinkled at knees, and my mind returns to how amazing he looked from behind as we came up the stairs.

And where did *that* thought come from? Since when did I notice Gabe's butt?

Shaking my head to clear the craziness from my brain, I look up into his startling blue eyes. "She still has her cashier job at a sporting goods store, so at least she's not unemployed. It's not great pay, but it's always been steady. When she called today, she sort of rambled about how her paycheck just wasn't going as far and her hours were less than usual, and she couldn't make her rent payment anymore."

"She's been evicted?"

"I don't think so," I say, but honestly, I'm not sure. Mom had been so vague on the phone that it was difficult to piece together exactly what the problem was.

"But she asked if she could move in with me for a few months while she worked on her finances. She said she could help with groceries and some of the rent."

I let my head fall back on the cushion and close my eyes. I love my mom. Like, for real. She went through hell several times over to give me a good life. But there's a reason kids move out and don't live with their parents once they become adults.

"How long have you been on your own?" Gabe asks.

"Three years." I sit up and turn toward him. He seems even closer than he was before, I shut my eyes, and my belly does a strange fluttery thing. "Since I graduated from high school."

"I get it," he says. "When I came to Flagstaff after high school, I stayed in the dorm even though my mom lives here."

That statement tells me so much about him. He's not from here. His parents must be divorced, because he doesn't mention his father, and evidently he didn't live with his mom before graduating high school. I'm surprised to realize that I'd like to know every detail about all of that, but I decide to stick with something safe.

"You went to NAU?" I ask.

Gabe nods.

"What did you study?"

He chuckles. "Well, *study* probably isn't the right term for what I did. At least not at first."

"Party too much?" I smile, thinking of Gabe as one

of those party-obsessed college freshmen.

"Not exactly. I was just kind of unmotivated and lazy." He picks up a strand of my dark hair and absently twirls it around his finger. I swear my hair must have nerve endings because I feel it in the center of my chest.

"I was a business major for almost two years," he goes on. "But I hated it. Middle of my sophomore year, I got a job here and loved it. That's when I dropped my major and just did a certificate in Entrepreneurship."

"It must've paid off, seeing as you're the manager now."

"How'd this conversation get derailed?" he asks with a grin while tugging gently on my hair. "We were talking about you, not me."

"I'm not nearly that interesting," I say. "I didn't even try college. Just went straight to work for Bing and learned on the job."

"No better way to learn. And you keep Resolution running smooth, so you must've learned fast."

Resolution is the tattoo shop where I work as receptionist and bookkeeper. Brett Channing, or Bing as he's known to practically everyone, is the owner. He, along with the other tattoo artists, Shane, Caleb, and Asher, are the best colleagues I could ever imagine. I love my job, and I love them.

For a moment, I'm tempted to tell Gabe the truth about how I came to work for Bing, but that's a story for another time.

"So," he says when my silence goes on a bit too long.

"Is your place big enough for your mom and you?"

I sigh. "It is, but it's not. I'll have to move some stuff around, but yeah, it'll work."

"I have an idea!" he says, leaping up from the couch and jogging to the kitchen. He rifles through a kitchen drawer for a moment until his hand closes around whatever it is he's searching for.

When he returns to the sofa, I can't see what's in his hand. He holds up his closed fist and says, "This is your escape."

I'm confused and about to ask what he's talking about when he reaches for my right hand. Turning it palm up, he opens his fist and places the small object in my hand, then closes my fingers around it. For a moment he holds my hand in both of his, his thumbs rubbing gently along the underside of my wrist. The sensation zings up my arm and straight to my heart, and I begin to wonder how all of a sudden Gabe Jenkins and his blond hair and witty humor has turned into this heart-palpitatingly romantic guy.

When I open my hand I see a key. A hundred thoughts run through my head in the space of about a second. Things like... *Is this some kind of symbolic thing? Am I supposed to wear it like a piece of jewelry?* And the scariest one of all... *Did he just give me a key to his apartment?*

"Gabe," I whisper. "I don't..."

"Don't freak out," he interrupts. "Yes, that's a key to my apartment. No, it's not what you're thinking. Unless you want it to be." He winks and his lips spread into that signature, playful Gabe smile. "Seriously, living with your mom again is going to test your patience, no matter how well the two of you get along. You're going to need some place to crash for an hour or two, when it gets to be too much. Some place where no one will ask questions. Some place you can just *be* for a while."

"Here?"

"Why not?" he asks. "Nobody's ever here but me, and I'm downstairs more often than I'm here. You can have some privacy when you need it. And if I happen to be up here, I already know what's up, so I won't bombard you with questions."

With his words, all the tension I've been carrying since Mom's phone call this morning ebbs away. Somehow, he's gotten right to the heart of what I'm feeling without me even realizing it and given me a measure of peace about it all.

"Okay," I whisper.

He smiles. His crystal blue eyes lock on mine. And that's when I know.

There is more to Gabe Jenkins than I've ever imagined.

Chapter 3

GABE

T HERE'S AN EXTRA skip in my step this morning as I
head downstairs. We open an hour later on Satur-
days, but things are already up and running by the time I
hit the kitchen. That's the benefit of having a dependable
weekend staff. I take a moment to appreciate the calm
morning and the staff who opened up so I didn't have to,
because without all the college employees, who won't be
back until the semester starts in a couple of weeks, I'll be
logging more hours this week than usual.

I'm just about to grab some coffee for myself when
the front door opens and Grace walks in, bringing a gust
of August air into the room.

"What are you doing here?" I ask, knowing she's not
on the schedule for today.

"I left my phone behind the counter last night," she
says. "Asher and I are headed back to Greyson for the
day, so I swung by here to pick it up before we get
going."

"Cool. Hope you guys have a nice visit with the
families."

At the cash register, Grace leans over and reaches beneath the counter, finding her phone where she'd stashed it last night. I make my way to a couple of tables greeting several thirty-something women, Ugly Mug's typical Saturday morning clientele. Even without summer break, the college kids don't roll out of bed at this hour a Saturday.

"So, I noticed you had a visitor up at your place last night," Grace says, stepping behind me and speaking low enough that no one else hears.

"We talked for a while." I shrug, trying to keep it nonchalant. I'm not the kind of guy to kiss and tell. Not that Rachelle and I had locked lips or anything, but we'd hung out, and it was cool, but it wasn't something I was talking about with Grace. "No big."

"Mmmm hmmm." Grace raises her eyebrows. "You think I haven't noticed you paying special attention to her every time she comes in?"

"I'm good to my friends." I head toward the kitchen, thinking about the copious amounts of caffeine in my immediate future.

"You don't personally deliver coffee to anyone else, Gabe." She stops me with a hand on my arm. "It's okay to admit she's special. Because she is."

I close my eyes and take a deep breath. No use trying to evade Grace. She's too perceptive.

"She is," I admit. "I just don't think she takes me seriously when I try to show her how special she is."

"She's got a tough exterior," Grace says. "But I think

that's just to protect the tender heart that's underneath."

"Yeah, well, if the guys at Resolution catch on to the fact that I've got my eyes on her, I'll never hear the end of it, so do me a favor and keep this between us."

"They won't hear it from me," Grace agrees, taking a step toward the door. "But it's all over your face. You can't keep it a secret forever."

"Just until Rach gets on board with me," I say with a wink, backing in the direction of the kitchen for the coffee I still haven't managed to get.

Chapter 4

Rachelle

"**A** HUNDRED FIFTY is the lowest I can go," says the woman on the other end of the phone.

The price for a decent twin size bed and mattress is actually lower than I expected, but I had to at least try to talk her down a bit. The twenty-five dollars she knocked off the original price is nothing to sneeze at.

"I'll take it," I reply, glad that I've been able to stay within Mom's budget so far. Rather than pay a mover to bring what little furniture she owns to my place or pay for a storage unit, I'd suggested she just sell her things and use the money to buy the few things she needed. Whatever money was leftover she could save and put toward her savings or a new place. Plus, it's not like we had room for two sofas or kitchen tables in my little duplex anyway.

"You'll pick it up yourself, right?" the woman asks. "That price don't include no delivery."

I shake my head. You can always count on online yard sale merchants for stellar grammar.

I hadn't thought about how to get the bed to my

place, but Caleb drives a pick-up and I figure I can get him to help me out.

"Yeah, sure." I glance at the appointment list, noting that Caleb isn't with a client right now. "Let me talk to my friend who's going to help me, and I'll give you a call back. We can set up a time."

I end the call on my cell phone, then pick up the shop phone and buzz Caleb's room, hoping he's back from lunch.

"What's up, Rach?" he answers.

"I need a favor," I begin. "I just bought a new bed for my apartment, and I need a truck to pick it up. I was hoping you could go with me to get it, then maybe help me move the treadmill and desk out of my second bedroom so I can move the bed in."

"Yeah, I can do that." The face that he agrees so quickly warms my heart. These guys may look rough around the edges with their ink and piercings, but they're the kindest people I've ever known. "When?"

"Tonight some time," I answer, looking at the appointments for the day. "Your last client is at seven, so let me call the woman I'm buying it from and arrange it for some time after that."

"Sounds good."

"Thanks, Caleb. I really appreciate it."

I hang up and swivel in my chair to find Bing leaning on the door facing of his office. Clearly, he'd been listening.

"What do you need an extra bed for?"

GABE'S SECRET

I take a deep breath. I've kept this from him on purpose because it just brings up stuff neither one of us wants to deal with, but I can't avoid telling him forever, and now that he's overheard, I may as well get it over with.

"My mom is moving in with me," I say, keeping my voice low in case anyone else in the shop is around. "Temporarily."

He says nothing, just raises his eyebrows.

"She's having some financial issues."

"Does he have anything to do with it?"

The word *he* comes out with all kinds of contempt. No surprise.

"Not that I know of." I roll my chair back from the counter and walk toward him. "We haven't heard from him in such a long time, I doubt he'd surface now. Apparently her hours have been cut, and she's having trouble making ends meet."

"That's not like her." It's a statement, not a question.

"I know," I say. "She's not freeloading or anything. She's promised to help with groceries and rent. She just can't swing it all on her own right now."

"Lots of folks finding themselves in that spot these days," Bing says with a nod. "I'll help you and Caleb get the bed moved and set up."

"Thanks." I nudge his arm with my shoulder just as the front door opens.

Gabe.

Chapter 5

GABE

FOR ABOUT HALF a second, Rachelle looks panicked that I might've overheard, but I see the moment she remembers that I already know. I don't let on that I do, because I'm sure she wants discretion.

"Asher around?" I ask. "I want to talk to him about some new ink."

Which is true enough. I do want some new work done. I just happened to come over here to talk to him about it rather than simply calling him or catching him sometime in Ugly Mug because I knew I'd run into Rachelle.

"He's finishing up with someone," she says. "You want to hang around and wait?"

Um… affirmative. Waiting means hanging out in the lobby with her.

"Sure."

"I've got a few drawings I need to finish up," Bing says, heading back into his workroom. "Buzz me if you need something."

The door clicks shut behind him, and I'm alone with

Rachelle. I don't even try to pretend I'm not happy about it. A smile spreads across my face, and with a wink I turn and grab a chair, moving it behind the counter to sit next to her.

"Only employees get to sit back here." She nudges me with her shoulder and grins. "But I guess I'll make an exception this time."

"I appreciate that." I nudge her back.

She's so beautiful it almost makes my heart hurt. Her black hair is piled on top of her head, some invisible thing not quite managing to contain the dark, wild strands. Several tendrils dangle down over her neck, laying softly against her bronze skin, and my fingers itch to reach out and touch them.

I refrain. Barely.

"New ink, huh?" she asks.

"Yeah, I have a few ideas I want to bounce off him. He did this star when he was apprenticing." I flip my arm over to show her the simple design a few inches above my wrist. "I want to turn it in to something more. Give him a chance to put his style into it." Since my chair doesn't swivel, I grab the arm of hers and turn her toward me. I lean close and lower my voice, just in case our voices should carry into Bing's room. "When's your mom get here?"

"Friday." She doesn't elaborate, and I can feel the mixed emotions churning inside her head. "Two more days of freedom."

"Well, you should make the most of them," I suggest. "Let me take you out. Dinner, dancing, maybe a movie."

She smiles, which was my intention. "I wish I could. Caleb's taking me to pick up a bed I just bought, then he and Bing are going to help me move it into my place."

"I'll come along. Another pair of hands can't hurt."

"You can't possibly want to spend the evening moving crap around my duplex."

"Why not?" I feign shock. "Nothing says romance like moving your mother in."

This time she laughs, and my heart smiles. "Okay."

"I'd suggest having dinner together tomorrow, but I have to work until closing. Ordinarily I'd just shuffle schedules around, but I'm a few people short until all the NAU students get back."

"Maybe I'll happen to come in for coffee." Her smile is hesitant, like she wonders if I want her to stop by.

Damn straight I do.

"Come by at closing. You can have your coffee and scone at my place."

She dips her head, then looks up at me through those impossibly long, dark eyelashes. I don't know what it is about women, if maybe that upward glance is some secret tool of seduction that they all learn in order to completely disarm defenseless men, but it's seriously working. I'm about two seconds away from rushing headlong into first base when Asher steps into the lobby, followed by the guy he just finished tattooing.

"You here to see me?" he asks.

Well, no. But that was my story, so I better stick to it.

All kinds of regret barrels through me as I stand up and move my chair back across the seating area. Not the least of which is the longing I see in Rachelle's eyes. The failed lip-lock mission seems to have affected her as much as it did me.

I head toward the hall with Asher, but turn back to Rachelle one last time.

"I'll be back here at seven to help you guys get things moved," I say with a wink.

She nods, one side of her mouth turning up in a smile.

And I feel like a million freaking bucks.

Chapter 6

RACHELLE

I MANAGE TO find a parking spot easily. With summer break winding down and most college kids still not back in town, the coffee shop isn't quite as packed as it normally be is.

It's thirty minutes before closing on my last night before Mom moves in, and I've chosen to spend it with Gabe. The truth of that isn't lost on me. That boy is working his way under my skin, and even though I can't decide if I like it or if I'm irritated by it, I'm here, which says a lot.

I like Gabe. I *like* Gabe.

I step in the front door and see him behind the counter working the espresso machine. Looks like he's on barista duty tonight.

And yeah… it's kind of hot.

All right… it's seriously hot.

Grace smiles at me from her spot at the cash register as I make my way to the counter.

Gabe is so intent on what he's doing, he doesn't see me approach. In fact, I'm plopped on a barstool admiring the huge variety of crazy mugs on the back wall before he notices me.

"Hey you!" he says, a huge smile lighting up his face. His messy blond hair is just a little too long, the ends curling up around his ears and the front falling almost to his eyebrow on the right side.

Yep, that's hot, too.

"Hi Gabe." What's with the nerves fluttering in my chest? It's not like I haven't been here for coffee a thousand times before. But this is the first time we've made actual plans to meet here, so in a way it's an *almost* date.

"Your usual?" he asks, referring to my normal hazelnut coffee and scone.

"Yes to the scone," I answer. "But instead of coffee, I'll take a dirty chai."

"Coming right up." He winks at me from behind the machine, and my stomach flips. Gabe is turning me to mush without even trying.

I reach for my wallet, but he stops me. "This one's on the house."

Part of me wants to protest, but he looks so happy to be treating me to chai and a scone. So I just smile and say, "Okay."

I watch as he fills the two orders ahead of mine, a vanilla latte and cappuccino, then grabs a to-go cup. The spicy scent of chai wafts through the air as he pours the espresso shot in and tops it with steamed milk.

"Hey Grace," Gabe says, popping the top on my cup

and grabbing the black marker. "You good to close up with Harrison?"

"Of course," she answers, sliding me a small bag that I assume holds my scone. "We got this."

"Thanks. I owe you."

"Yes, several times over," Grace teases.

Gabe continues writing on my cup, which is strange since I'm sitting right here. It's not like I'm going to accidentally grab the wrong drink.

"Ready to head upstairs?"

I nod, and we walk toward the back of the building. Gabe carries my drink while I carry the scone, so I still have no idea what he wrote on my cup.

When we get to the top of the steps, he hands the cup to me so he can dig his key from his pocket and unlock the door. I wait until he's turned toward the door to look at the writing.

And my heart lodges in my throat.

The most beautiful girl in the world.

He pushes the door open and looks back, seeing me staring at his words. Speech escapes me. Do I say thank you? Do I brush it off as flattery?

Gabe saves me from my awkwardness when he brings his hand to my face and lifts my chin.

"It's the truth," he says. "At least for me."

I fight urge to come completely undone right there at the door to his apartment and manage to hold on to my dignity by a thread.

Gabe Jenkins. What are you doing to me?

"Come on in." He smiles and gestures to the door, and I walk in ahead of him.

He heads straight for the couch and grabs the remote. As Jimmy Fallon comes to life on the TV screen, I take a seat next to him and sip my chai.

For the next hour, we laugh at Fallon and talk about lots of things, none of which are important or life-changing.

It's absolutely wonderful. I can't remember the last time I had this much fun, and I'm incredibly grateful for the way he's made me feel light and carefree the night before my life turns upside down.

"I should go." I stand up and collect my trash from his coffee table. "Big day tomorrow."

He clicks the TV off and pushes up of the couch. "You working all day?"

I shake my head. "Just until lunch. That's when Mom's supposed to be at my place."

"Need any help getting her moved in?" he asks, taking my empty cup and sack from my hands and walking to the kitchen trash.

"I don't think so." I follow him to the kitchen. "She's just moving in clothes and personal stuff. The hard work was the other night when you and the guys helped move the bed in." I take a deep breath and decide to be honest. "And I'm just not ready to make a social event of Mom moving in yet."

He puts his arms around me, like it's the most natural thing in the world. Just holds me and lets his warmth surround me. And suddenly I realize that for all my life I haven't believed men like him really exist.

I know better now.

He rests his chin on the top of my head and says, "I'm going to want to meet your mom eventually."

I chuckle. "Yeah, and I'm going to want to meet yours, too."

"Glad we established that." He releases me from his embrace, but takes my hand in his. "We'll plan a 'meet the parents' event for the near future."

"Thank you Gabe," I say as we walk toward the door. I hope he knows what I'm thanking him for because heaven knows there are too many things to name them all.

"Still got your key?" he asks, turning the knob to open the door.

"Yes."

"Use it whenever you need to."

"Aren't you worried I might barge in on you and a date?"

As soon as the words leave my mouth I want to punch myself in the face. Clearly, I'm just fishing around to see if he's seeing other girls, and that comment was my pathetic attempt to find out. Stupid, Rachelle.

But Gabe just laughs, completely unbothered. "Right, Rachelle. I've got a steady stream of women lined up at my door."

I just grin and shrug my shoulder. My way of apologizing for my stupid comment.

"You're the only girl coming and going from my place," he whispers, placing a soft kiss on my forehead. "As long as you want it that way."

I'm slightly disappointed that he didn't kiss me full-on, but there's a real sweetness to the way he showed affection in such a modest way, so I take the loveliness of that small kiss and hide it away in my heart.

"Okay," I whisper.

Chapter 7

GABE

THE WEEK OF all the NAU students' return is nuts, with college kids rolling back into Ugly Mug for the post-break debriefing. I'm finally calling it a night well after midnight. Despite the fact that we close at eleven, getting the twenty-somethings out the door at that hour is next to impossible when they're all still high on beach vacation memories.

I realize I sound like a grouchy old man, complaining about the twenty-somethings, when at twenty-two, I *am* a twenty-something.

I don't bother turning on the lights when I walk in my apartment. Instead, I just kick off my shoes and collapse on the couch. Rachelle flashes through my mind, like she does every minute of the day, so I pull out my phone and shoot her a text.

Me: *You still awake?*

I haven't seen Rachelle since the night before her mom moved in. I know she feels obligated to spend her spare time with her mom, at least for the first week or so, but holy cow, I've missed her. Our back and forth texting is just not cutting it.

My screen lights up with an incoming text.

Rachelle: *Yeah. Mom's been asleep for an hour, and I'm catching up on the DVR.*

I smile, imagining her curled up on the little green love seat in her tiny duplex.

Me: *Late night. You must not work in the morning.*

Rachelle: *I go in after lunch. You?*

Me: *Harrison's opening up. It's been a crazy couple of days, and I'm not rolling out of this apartment until I'm good and ready.*

Rachelle: *Sounds like a plan.*

Me: *I wish you were here.*

Good grief. Could I sound any more maudlin?

Rachelle: *Go to sleep, Gabe. You can imagine me there.*

Yeah, if she only knew.

Me: *We're gonna have to make it a reality soon.*

Rachelle: *I'll work on that tomorrow.*

I text her good night and head to bed. I drop my clothes on the floor, not bothering to throw them in the laundry basket, figuring I'll do it in the morning. As I plug my phone up to the charger, I see the notification indicating a new email, so I touch the icon to open it.

Immediately, I wish hadn't.

My grandmother. Sylvia Barlow Jenkins.

Gabriel,

It's your grandmother, in case you've forgotten. I would like to invite you to our Labor Day celebration at Hawthorne Place. All of your father's business associates will be there, as well as our friends on the board of the Children's Literacy Foundation. I hope you'll consider returning and being a part of your family once again.

I've just celebrated my seventy-second birthday, and at this age I never know which birthday will be my last. I would hope you might wish to see me again at least once, so that you won't have to live with the regret of turning your back on your family. As you know, your father recovered from a severe bout with pneumonia in the spring, which I contacted you about several times. Luckily, he is still feeling fine. I know you would've hated to lose him forever with such animosity still between you. It's up to you to make things right before it's too late.

Please contact me at your earliest convenience and let me know your travel plans for Labor Day. I'll be looking forward to your return.

No closing. Not a *sincerely* or an *all my love.* Just the standard signature that ends all of her emails.

Sylvia Barlow Jenkins.

My grandmother is famous in her social circle for the celebrations she throws. Not that she does the decorating or the cooking. Naturally, she hires people to do all the actual work. She just makes sure she looks impeccable as she welcomes people to Hawthorne Place, the sprawling Kansas City mansion where I spent the first eighteen years of my life. Those years were miserable, and I vowed to never go back.

I couldn't care less about the advertising business my grandfather built, and then handed down to my sorry excuse for a father. I want no part of it or the fortune it amassed.

I haven't touched one cent of the trust fund that became mine a year ago when I turned twenty-one. It feels like blood money, paid for with the misery and tears that my mother and I endured.

For the past year the fund has been legally mine, I've been pondering what to do with it. I've looked into lots of charities and non-profits, thinking maybe I could give it all away. But nothing seems quite right yet.

Mentally, I slam the door on my grandmother and her passive aggressive bitchiness and flop back down on my mattress. Sylvia Barlow Jenkins is banished from my thoughts in favor of a bronze-skinned, black-haired beauty that I can't get enough of. And probably never will.

Chapter 8

GABE

SOMEBODY'S IN MY apartment.

My mind realizes it a second or two before by body catches up, and in that brief moment of almost-consciousness, I conjure up all sorts of scenarios.

Someone is breaking in. But why? To steal my TV? It's not like there's a multitude of valuable stuff in here.

Maybe it's a rat digging through my trash. Even half-asleep I'm at myself enough to say a prayer that isn't the case. Marshall and Janie Lewis, Ugly Mug's owners, will have a serious meltdown if a rodent winds up in here.

And the worst-case scenario. Harrison has come up here with some kind of crisis that requires my immediate attention. I'll kill him. Like completely murder him.

Slipping quietly from the bed, I grab my jeans off the floor and pull them on. I zip them up, but forgo the button in favor of grabbing my phone in case I have to call 911. Or an exterminator.

I see a missed call from my grandmother, who I've just decided to refer to only as *Sylvia* since using her first name doesn't imply a family relationship. I don't a reminder about her invitation right before I go out there and face whatever is rifling through my kitchen.

Creeping through the living room, I hang close to the wall, thinking maybe I can sneak up on whoever – or whatever – it is. I peek around the corner into the kitchen area and see nothing. However, I hear something moving around on the floor behind the island. Great, it probably *is* a rat.

I tiptoe across toward the island, hoping to get a look at the intruder, when suddenly Rachelle stands up. When she sees me, she screams, and the napkins in her hands go flying.

"Gabe! You scared me to death!" she shrieks, her hands flying to her chest.

"Holy crap, Rachelle! What are you doing here?" I don't mean to shout, but I'm pretty sure that's how it came out. I'm also aware that I sound rather displeased by her presence.

Which isn't the case at all.

I'm just not quite awake yet, and if I'm honest, I'm still twisted up over *Sylvia's* email. God, just the thought of that woman and everything back in Kansas City makes me want to vomit.

"Making it a reality," she replies, her voice a soft whisper. She's calmer now that the shock of startling one another has passed, but I can see the wariness in her eyes, and I hate that my reaction caused that.

"Rach," I say, stepping toward her, still puzzled by her response.

My confusion must show on my face because she launches into an explanation. "Last night you said you wished I was here. I said you could imagine me here. You said we needed to make it a reality, and I told you I'd work on it tomorrow."

I remember. I'd enjoyed those few minutes of shameless flirting via text message. Before *Sylvia's* email.

She points across to the living room where I see two sub sandwiches from my favorite deli on the coffee table. "So I brought lunch. I thought we could eat together before work."

I should be wrapping my arms around her, apologizing, and thanking her. Instead, I stand there stunned and mute, trying without much success to get my brain to catch up with reality.

"I was just looking for napkins." She continues with her explanation. "I didn't mean to startle you awake."

I take a deep breath and close my eyes. Time to back this conversation up.

"Can I just start over?" I ask. When she nods, I keep going. "Hey Rachelle. I'm really glad you're here. I've missed you."

A smile spreads across her face, and I figure I'm forgiven. I pull her to me, put my arms around her, and press a kiss to the top of her head. She feels exactly right against me, the top of her head fitting perfectly under my chin, and there's no way to accurately describe the feeling of her arms snaking around my middle and squeezing tight.

I tell the ghost of Sylvia's email to leave me the hell alone so I can enjoy lunch with my girl.

Because she *is* my girl, whether she knows it yet or not.

Chapter 9

RACHELLE

IT HASN'T ESCAPED me that Gabe is shirtless. How could it with my face currently pressed against his bare chest? I've always liked the way Gabe looks. He's darn cute, and combined with his wacky personality, he's always been appealing.

But shirtless... wow. His six foot, two inch frame isn't body builder bulky, but rather lean and toned. His jeans hang low on his hips, and naturally I noticed the button was not fastened. I manage not to drool at the thought.

His skin is warm against my cheek, and his arms are secure around me, and I'm considering blowing off work just to stand here in his embrace all day long.

"What kind of sandwich is that?" he asks.

I lean back and smile up at him. "The triple meat Italian, plus bacon."

"Seriously?" His face lights up. "How'd you know?"

"Shane," I answer. "I called and pretended I was getting lunch for Mom and me. I got him talking about your last video game night, and he spilled your favorite

"Smart girl." He unravels himself from me and grabs my hand. "Let's eat."

He retrieves two cans of root beer from the fridge while I gather the napkins I dropped earlier, and the two of us settle on the couch and dig in.

"Sorry I yelled at you earlier," Gabe says, grabbing the second half of his sandwich. "I thought you might be a rat."

"A rat?" I ask, laughing and somehow managing not to choke.

"Remember that I wasn't even half awake yet. I was just imaging how freaked out Marshall and Janie were going to be if we'd been infested with rodents."

I polish off half of my sandwich and wrap the other half to stick in Gabe's refrigerator before I leave. "Are Marshall and Janie the owners?"

"Yeah. They're great. They own a shop in Phoenix, too, but they travel a lot now that both their kids are grown, so they have managers at both places to keep things running."

"And you rent this place from them?" I ask, reaching for my drink.

"I would," he answers. "But it's part of my salary. The woman who runs the Phoenix shop lives above it, too. I think it gives them some peace of mind knowing someone's always around to take are of things."

"I guess it's convenient for you, too."

"Yes and no. The commute to work is awesome." He

grins and winks. "But it also means anytime something goes wrong, rather than just trying to handle it, Harrison or one of the others just calls me or runs up here."

I glance at my phone and realize I have to be at Resolution in twenty minutes. The disappointment I feel at the thought of leaving Gabe is both frightening and exciting.

"Before I go, I wanted to ask you something," I say, grabbing my unfinished sandwich half and walking over to his kitchen. "You said something about wanting to meet my mom, and since Labor Day is next week, I thought maybe we could have lunch together on Sunday, since neither one of us works that day. You could invite your mom, too, if you wanted."

Even from across the room, I can see his shoulders slump, like he feels defeated by the idea of meeting my mom for Sunday lunch. And now that I think about it, he's been a little *off* today, like something's bothering him but he doesn't want to talk about it.

"If you have plans, it's fine," I say, quickly backpedaling to give him an out if he wants it. I won't deny I'll be disappointed, but I don't want to force the issue. "We can do it another time."

"It's not that," he says, running his hand through his hair. I can sense the frustration rolling off him as he stands, wads up his trash, and heads toward the kitchen to throw it away. "I don't have plans. I'm just…"

He stops mid-sentence, and I say nothing. I have no idea how we got this derailed, and I'm completely unsure how to proceed.

His sandwich wrapper lands in the trash, and he takes a deep breath before turning to me. "You know what? I'd love that. There's no other way I'd rather spend a Sunday afternoon than with you and our moms."

The expression on his face doesn't exactly match the enthusiasm in his words, but I let it go. Maybe the thought of actually meeting my mom makes him nervous. And if it's something else… well, everybody finds themselves in a funk sometimes. I'm sure he'll work his way out.

"Great." I take a chance and step toward him, taking his hand in mind. "Do you have a favorite restaurant? Or is there a place your mom particularly likes?"

His eyebrows shoot up and a giant smile appears on his face. Just like that, cheerful Gabe is back. "I have an idea!"

I return his smile, going with the flow of his returning joviality. "Let's hear it."

"Ugly Mug is closed this Sunday. Why not have lunch here? Downstairs. I can even cook!"

"You cook?" He seems genuinely excited about this possibility.

"Of course I cook! I don't just survive on coffee, muffins, and sandwiches beautiful girls bring me."

I can't help but laugh. Whatever had him concerned a moment ago seems long gone and not worth worrying over.

He keeps going. "I mean, it won't be five courses of

gourmet stuff, but I can put something good together."

"Why don't we cook together?" I suggest. "We'll get here an hour or so before we tell our moms to arrive and put it all together ourselves."

"Perfect!"

He grabs my other hand and pulls me to him, a playful grin on his face. His head tilts to the side as he starts to lean forward, and I think *finally* he's going to kiss me.

I'm about to close my eyes and sink into that sweet moment of anticipation when a loud banging commences at the door.

"Gabe!" Harrison's voice shouts. "We got a problem downstairs!"

Gabe's head drops to my shoulder, and I feel him shaking with laughter. Not the *ha-ha* funny type of laughter, but the kind that says, *Can you believe this?*

"See what I mean?" he asks, turning his head and placing a light kiss against my neck.

"Always on call," I answer.

"Be right down," he calls to Harrison. Then to me, he whispers, "Sorry."

I shake my head, letting him know it's fine. "Don't worry. I need to get over to Resolution. You go put out the fire, Captain." I wink at him before grabbing my purse from the counter and walking toward the door. "But put on a shirt and button your pants first."

I hear his laughter as I shut the door behind me and head down the stairs.

Chapter 10

GABE

CRISIS AVERTED. HARRISON hasn't mastered the fine art of unjamming the cash register drawer, which caused a bit of mild panic when a customer needed change for a hundred dollar bill.

Back up in my apartment, I smile at the memory of finding Rachelle in my kitchen and the sweetness of her gesture. She didn't just surprise me with lunch. She practically admitted she's into me.

And yeah... I'm happy about that.

I know I let my face slip when she mentioned Labor Day weekend. I could tell in the way she hurried to make it seem like her invitation was no big deal. I couldn't let her think I didn't want to spend the day with her and our moms. It's not like I had any intention of going back to Kansas City anyway.

Rather than just ignore Sylvia like I usually do, I decide to call her and put this to rest once and for all. I know it will be unpleasant, but I'm tired of dancing around the issue. My life in Kansas City is over, and she's just going to have to get used to it.

I pull out my phone and dial, simultaneously dreading the conversation and looking forward to the relief I'll feel when it's over. A voice in the back of my mind whispers that I should tell Rachelle the truth about my family in Kansas City. Or rather about the *people* in Kansas City that I once had to deal with. They aren't my family, anymore. I want to tell her. I really do. But my past is so ugly. I convince myself that if I give her a little more time to get to know me better, the truth won't scare her away.

"Gabriel." Sylvia picks up on the fourth ring.

I shake my head. She's always refused to call me Gabe. "Sylvia."

The use of her first name instead of the expected *grandmother* catches her off guard and grants me a small moment of silence before she launches into her speech.

"I'm certainly glad you called," she beings. "When will you be flying in? I'll make arrangements for a car to pick you up at the airport, and I'll have housekeeping make sure your room is fresh and ready for your arrival. Your father's associates are so anxious to see you again."

When she pauses to take a breath, I interrupt. "I'm not coming, Sylvia. Not this time, and not ever again."

"I'm sure you don't mean that, Gabriel." Classic Sylvia. Ignore reality and pretend things are exactly as you want them to be.

"I do mean it," I say. "I've been gone for four years. I haven't been back yet, and I have no plans to ever come back. Please, just accept that and stop contacting me."

Sylvia scoffs. "Nonsense. This is your home. Your family is here."

"My home is here." I can't help the clip in my voice. Sylvia always brings it out in me. "In Arizona. And so is my family."

She sighs, and I know the drill. She's going to pretend to understand and act like she's making some giant concession by agreeing with me.

"I know your mother is there, but you surely haven't forgotten that you spent your formative years at Hawthorne Place."

I laugh out loud. Her statement is so ridiculous that I can't stop myself.

"As if I could ever forget one miserable moment of growing up in that hell hole. Of course I haven't forgotten, Sylvia, which is the exact reason that I'm never coming back."

"But your father," she begins. I cut her off before she can continue.

"He's not my father," I practically shout into the phone. I can't find it in myself to feel bad about it. "He never was, and he sure as hell isn't anymore. And he can rot in that prison cell for the rest of his life."

With that, I click to hang up and fall onto the couch. I'm exhausted… and exhilarated.

Chapter 11

RACHELLE

I'M SITTING AT the front counter of Resolution Ink, finishing up my work for the day, when my phone vibrates beside me. My shift is over in thirty minutes, and since Mom gets off work each day at three o'clock, I know she's calling to make dinner plans.

She's done it every single day. Every. Single. Day.

It's been just over week, and I'm losing my mind.

There's a fair amount of guilt running around in my head, berating me about how much I'm *not* enjoying Mom living with me. On one hand, there's the fact that she's my mom and I love her. I want to help her out. On the other hand, there's the fact that I've been living on my own for three years. I'm used to my space and being able to come and go without explanation.

Add to that the way Mom's still being evasive and refusing to give me specifics about her financial problems, and I'm already reaching my limit in this situation. She says she doesn't want me to worry about her... that it's not my job to concern myself with her money issues. However, I think giving her a place to live while she straightens things out entitles me to a bit more information.

With a heavy sigh, I grab my phone and swipe to answer the call.

"Hi Mom."

"Rachelle, I've got a great idea!" Her voice sing-songs across the phone. "How long before you get home?"

"I've got about thirty minutes left here," I answer. "But Mom—"

"I picked up a package of those egg rolls that you love so much," she says, interrupting whatever objection I'd been about to mutter. "I'll start cooking them so they'll be ready when you get home. One of the premium cable channels is running free promotion this weekend, so there are lots of movies to choose from."

I love egg rolls. Truly. And I love free HBO weekends. But the level of *oh please no* I feel at the prospect of going home tonight is staggering. I decide in that instant that I've got to take a break. Not because I'm mad at Mom or because I want her to go. But because I don't want to say something or act in a way I'll regret.

Just one night… one dinner and a TV show. That's all I need to refresh and recharge. A plan forms in my head and I go with it.

"Mom, I kind of have plans with a friend," I tell her, even though I just made those plans five seconds ago. "It just sort of came up recently."

I wait for her response, afraid I've hurt her feelings. Crap. Not what I meant to do at all.

"Of course you do. It's Friday night." When she laughs, I let out a breath of relief. "I should've realized. I know you must have a social life, and I've completely monopolized your time."

"It's okay, Mom," I reassure her. "I love spending time with you. I just, well —"

"You want to be a normal, twenty-one year-old woman," she says. "I get it. Go ahead. There's plenty on TV, and we can have egg rolls tomorrow."

"You're not a bother, Mom." Despite needing a breather, I want her to know this. "At all."

"Thanks, honey." Her voice goes soft, in that way only moms can do. "I appreciate that. But I hope you know that you don't have to revolve your life around me just because I'm staying with you for a while."

"Tomorrow night," I say, hoping she can hear my smile across the phone line. "Egg rolls and movies."

"Deal."

Chapter 12

GABE

I'M SO GRATEFUL *not* to be working this Friday night, so why the heck am I standing in the kitchen of Ugly Mug at six o'clock?

But I know why. Because it's been two days since I've seen Rachelle. She's still trying to be sensitive to her mom, and I get that. But damn, I miss her.

Grace breezes into the kitchen grabbing a few clean saucers and utensils to put out front with the pastry shelves. She eyes me with curiosity because she knows I'm not on the schedule for tonight.

"No Rachelle tonight?" she asks as she walks past.

I shake my head and follow her to the counter where the clean dishes are stacked.

"Still hanging out with her mom in the evenings?" She begins counting plates, preparing what she needs to take to the front.

"Trying to navigate how to go back to living under the same roof with her, I guess."

"Can't be easy," Grace replies, picking up the dishes but making no move to step away. "I've only been away for a year, and I don't know how I'd deal. Not that I don't get along with my folks, but I sort of feel like I've grown up and learned how to take care of myself."

I nod. Grace is a surprisingly mature young lady. At nineteen years old, she's almost done with cosmetology school, which she's completing while working a pretty hefty part-time schedule here. And she's in a serious, committed relationship with Asher Howell, my buddy who used to work here with me and now tattoos full time at Resolution.

Which is how I met Rachelle. Life works in circles, I guess.

"Rach loves her mom," I say. "But I figure it's kind of like being a kid again, wondering if you have a curfew or if you have to ask permission."

"She'll figure it out, I'm sure." She starts to walk away, then stops and turns around again. "Best I can tell, Asher and the guys don't know yet. Are you two official yet?"

"We haven't been out on a date yet." I shrug my shoulders. "But in my mind, we're official. She did suggest that we get together Labor Day weekend... with our moms."

Grace nods. "Sounds official to me. Let me know when the guys at Resolution find out. I'm sure they'll be fine about it, but if you need me to run interference, I can do it."

"Thanks," I say, smiling. Grace is a top-notch friend.

My thoughts turn back to my empty Friday night

agenda, once again wishing Rachelle and I could be together. As I run my schedule for the rest of the weekend over in my head, I remember that she mentioned being off work on Saturday, which means maybe we can manage lunch together tomorrow.

My grocery supply is pretty lousy, so I figure I better stock up before I invite Rachelle over. Reaching in my pocket for my keys, I head out the back door.

Chapter 13

Rachelle

G ABE'S CAR IS not in its usual spot behind Ugly Mug. I scold myself for the wayward jealous thought that runs through my head... wondering if he's out with friends... or another girl.

I don't want to immediately assume the worst about him. Not all men are assholes like my father. Not all men lie and cheat and abuse. Some men are kind and generous and treasure their loves ones.

It's time to start putting Gabe in *that* category first.

He told me there would be no more girls as long as I wanted it that way. I need to believe him.

I notice Grace's car and decide to make sure it's okay to slip up to his apartment while he's not home. Leaving my car in the back lot, I make my way to the kitchen door and step in carefully, hoping to avoid colliding with a hot cup of coffee.

The kitchen is busy, like it always is on Friday nights, whipping up sandwiches and salads for the college crowd. Harrison is manning the espresso machine while Grace works the counter and pastry cabinet. Slipping quietly from the chaos in the kitchen, I make my way to her. A break in the line gives me an opportunity to bend her ear.

"Hi Rachelle." Grace's warm smile always makes me feel at ease. Asher certainly hit the jackpot with this girl. "Gabe just left a few minutes ago."

"Any idea when he's coming back?" I ask, hoping I don't sound over-anxious.

"He said he was going to do a little shopping," Grace answers. "I assume he was going for groceries, but I'm not sure."

"Do you think it would be okay if I waited upstairs for him?" I know he said to use the key he gave me anytime, but I can't help but wonder if I'd be intruding.

"I'm sure he wouldn't mind." She reaches under the register and pulls a key from a hook that must be hidden between the cash drawer and the side of the counter. "His emergency key."

She holds it out to me, and I realize that I hadn't thought about telling her I already have a key. What exactly is she going to think about the situation if she knows I have one? Will she jump to the wrong conclusion? Should I just take the emergency key and pretend, or let Grace in on the fact that I can come and go from Gabe's apartment anytime?

Not wanting to be secretive – and figuring if anyone can be trusted to not make assumptions it's Grace – I tell her the truth.

"I have a key," I whisper. "He gave it to me in case I

needed a place to get away for a while, you know, after Mom moved in."

"He's a thoughtful one," she says. "Not everyone sees it because he's always joking around, but he's got a sweet heart."

A sweet heart. A very apt description of the Gabe I'm coming to know.

"He does," I agree. "I'm going to slip upstairs and hang out until he gets home."

"If he comes through here first, I won't say a word." She hangs the key back in its hiding spot and grins. "He'll be surprised."

I smile back, glad she and I had this talk. It'll be good to have her stamp of approval once the guys at the shop find out Gabe and I are seeing each other. Not that Bing or the others have ever done the over-protective thing, but still. Having Grace on my side will quell any objections the guys might raise.

Walking back through the bustling kitchen, I push my way through the door that leads to the stairway. I dig the key from my purse and turn the lock. Even though I used it a few days ago when I surprised him with lunch, I'm still a bit surprised when it works, still a little astounded that he trusts me enough to share his home with me this way.

These are the things I need to remember when I think of Gabe. His trust. His thoughtfulness. His sweet heart.

I grab the remote from the coffee table and get comfy on the couch. Flipping through the channels, I stop when I land on BBC and an episode of *Doctor Who*. It's "The Eleventh Hour", Matt Smith's debut as the Doctor, and one of my favorite episodes. Smiling, I settle in to wait for Gabe's return.

Chapter 14

GABE

THE TV IS on when I open the door. I didn't leave it on. Although, I've been known to binge a bit on *Doctor Who*, I know for a fact I haven't been watching BBC today.

I drop my groceries by the door and make my way to the sofa.

And my heart turns over in my chest.

Rachelle is curled up in the corner of the couch, sound asleep.

Her dark hair spreads out over the cushions, and her pretty bronze skin is highlighted by the bright coral color of her shirt. Her hands are tucked beneath her cheek, and her face looks so serene and peaceful.

She's so beautiful it makes me ache.

A few hours ago I was complaining about not having enough time with her. Now here she is, asleep on my couch.

I sit down on the coffee table and lean across to her. Gently, I place my palm against her cheek, letting my thumb stroke soft circles beneath her eye. I want her to know I'm here, but I also don't want to startle her awake. That's unpleasant, as we both learned the other day.

Tonight she's wearing a stud with a tiny pink stone in her nose, and a larger one that matches below her lip. Some people might find facial piercings on a girl strange or distracting, but to me, they're sparkling and feminine... just like her.

Rachelle doesn't do body modification for attention anyway. She's just herself. And I love that about her.

"Hey Rach," I whisper as her eyes start to flutter open.

She blinks a few times then sits up with a jolt. "I fell asleep."

"Yeah." I can't help but chuckle.

"I'm sorry."

"For what?" I ask, reaching over to take her hands. "For showing up in my apartment and making my night a whole lot better?"

She smiles and lowers her eyes. "Does it make me an awful daughter that I just couldn't go home tonight?"

"Of course not." I shake my head. "I'm sure your mom understands."

Rachelle nods her head. "She does."

"You know, I was going to invite you over for lunch tomorrow, but since you're here, how about dinner?"

"Dinner?" she asks.

"Yeah, you know that meal you eat about this time every night? I've just been to the store, and I came home with plenty of groceries. You just keep enjoying *Doctor*

Who, and I'll cook."

❖   ❖   ❖

OF COURSE, RACHELLE doesn't just sit and watch TV while I cook. She insists on helping. I'd be lying if I said I wasn't enjoying the way she brushes up against me when she reaches for a knife or the way she stands super close as she watches me stir fry the broccoli and mushrooms.

Thirty minutes later we've got chicken stir fry and fried rice. I admit that I cheated and bought prepackaged fried rice that only required microwaving. Because, face it, cooking rice takes too long.

Rather than eating on the sofa like I usually do, I set two places at the bar on the kitchen island, and we each take a seat on a barstool.

"David Tennant or Matt Smith?" I ask, inquiring which actor's portrayal of *Doctor Who* she prefers.

"Tough choice because I like them both," she answers, pausing to think. "And I liked Christopher Eccleston, too. But if I had to pick one, it would be Matt Smith. I like quirky guys." She adds the last line with a wink.

Over dinner, we continue with light-hearted conversation and lots of laughter. Discovering we have so much in common – a love of *Doctor Who,* Chinese food, and old school jazz – is an added bonus.

"This is a pretty great first date," she says, helping me load the dishwasher.

"It's not really a date," I reply. "But I definitely want to take you out on a real one soon."

"I'd like that." She nudges me with her shoulder and points between the kitchen and the TV. "But this was definitely a date. We had dinner and entertainment."

An idea occurs to me, and I can't help the smile that spreads across my face. Taking her hand, I walk over and grab the remote to shut off the TV, then take my phone from my pocket and head to the small speaker on the shelf.

"Now all we need is dancing."

Chapter 15

RACHELLE

WHEN FRANK SINATRA'S voice slides smoothly from the speaker, my heart melts into a liquid mess of romance and emotion. Gabe wasn't kidding about his love for classic jazz.

"Is that a whole playlist of Sinatra?" I ask as he walks toward me holding out his hand.

"It is." He takes my hand and pulls me to him, his other hand settling on the small of my back. Lifting our clasped hands to his lips, he places a kiss on my fingers before beginning to sway gently to the music.

Gabe sings along, and so do I, and over the course of several songs he spins me around the living room like a pro. I love this side of him, the fun-loving, wacky guy who can turn any situation into something to smile about. But then the music slows, and our laughter turns to soft, sweet gazes, as Gabe pulls me against him.

"I love this one," he whispers, his lips grazing my ear.

"Me too." I lay my head against his chest and snuggle close as the melody of *When My Heart Stood Still* floats from the speaker.

The air around us changes; becomes charged with a feeling of hyperawareness. I'm focused on every move he makes, every breath he takes. The press of his hand on my back becomes heavier. His breath against my ear becomes warmer.

Unclasping the hands we have twined together, he slides his fingers into the hair at the back of my neck. I lift my head to look at him just as his other hands moves from my back to come to rest against my neck. My breath stops... backing up into my lungs as I stare into his bright blue eyes.

It's that moment of anticipation, when the excitement of knowing what's coming but not knowing what it will be like consumes every molecule in your body. Part of me wants to stay right here, in this moment, for the rest of my life, but a bigger, stronger part wants desperately to finally know the feel of Gabe's lips on mine.

And as the Sinatra's words ring out – about a man taking one look at a woman and his heart standing still – Gabe finally lowers his head.

The first press of his mouth is tender, a gentle brush of lips that steals my breath and makes my heart stutter. And then he sinks deeper into the kiss, tilting my head to the side and urging my lips open. Carefree Gabe is nowhere to be found, but in-charge Gabe is all over me.

The other day when I was disappointed that he didn't kiss me after Harrison's interruption? Yeah, I'm not complaining anymore. I can't imagine anything more amazing than *this* first kiss.

I snake my arms around his back, my hands kneading the muscles there. His hands finally leave my neck so that his arms can wrap me up in their strength. I have no idea how long we stand there tangled up together. The song changes several times, but neither of us pays attention.

Everything else just fades away in the maelstrom of Gabe's kiss.

The kiss slows, and gradually Gabe pulls back, just enough so he can look at me. He leaves our foreheads and noses pressed together and then smiles, his blue eyes sparkling in the afterglow.

"*Now* it's officially a date," he says with a grin.

I giggle softly and feel his arms tighten around me.

He shakes his head and his expression turns slightly serious. "I don't want to make a joke of this, or make it seem less than it is," he whispers. "I've been looking at you for so long, Rachelle, and now... being able to hold you and kiss you... it's not something to make light of. It's *everything*."

I feel something turning and squeezing in my chest, trying to make room for the weight of his words. Gabe's attention and affection have been so unexpected that my long-dormant heart is stretching in places it never expected. And yet, the feeling is more welcoming than anything I've ever known.

"You should've said something sooner," I whisper back.

One corner of his mouth turns up in a sheepish smile as his lids lower. "I know I probably seem pretty sure of myself, with the joking around and all that. And in many ways, I am confident and easygoing, but when it comes to this," he says, placing his palm over his heart. "Well, let's just say I had an entire childhood to perfect the art of keeping what was in here hidden. Bringing it out into the open is a little scary, but with you, I just couldn't wait any longer."

Wow. Part of me wants to find out what he meant about his childhood, but more than that, I don't want to ruin the absolute beauty of this moment.

"Well, thank you," I say, bringing my hand up and placing it over his, where it still rests on the left side of his chest. "For trusting me with this. I'll take care of it."

He kisses me again, our hands trapped between us, and I'm lost. Lost in a whirlwind of something I don't even recognize… something I never want to leave.

Chapter 16

GABE

I DON'T KNOW how long it's been since the music stopped, but somewhere in the middle of that last kiss, my Sinatra playlist finished and my phone went silent. Still standing in the same spot, wrapped up tight in each other, Rachelle pulls back and checks the time.

A heavy sigh leaves her. "I should probably go."

I knew she'd eventually go home, but damn. I've never wanted to freeze time more than I do right now.

"Yeah, I was afraid of that." I deliver the line with a smile, so she'll know I'm cool with it, even though I feel like I might not be able to breathe once she's gone.

"Tonight was," she stops and closes her eyes. "I can't even begin to tell you."

I slide my hand up to her neck and pull her gently to me until her head is resting against my chest. Leaning down just enough, I put my lips against her ear and whisper, "I know."

I know if we stand here another minute she might never leave. The better half of me wins out, and I take her hand and walk her to the door.

"I'll walk you out," I say, helping her slip her jacket on. I've walked her out before when she's left my apartment after dark, but tonight it seems bigger, more significant. The need to protect her has rocketed up to enormous proportions.

Hand in hand, we make our way down the steps and out the back door. The back lot is empty except for Harrison's car. I assume he's finishing up inside, getting Ugly Mug closed down for the night. Rach pulls her keys from her purse and unlocks her Ford Focus with the remote.

I reach down and open her door, but before she gets in, she turns back to me.

"Thank you again." She reaches up and fiddles with the strand of my hair that falls across my eye. "For dinner and… everything."

I lean into her, placing a soft kiss against her lips. For my own sanity, I don't deepen it because I might not make it out of the parking lot alive if I do.

"I'll call you tomorrow," I say, watching as she slips into the driver's seat. "We'll make plans for Labor Day weekend."

She nods, but doesn't start the car. Neither one of us is in a hurry for this night to end, and together we're doing just about everything we can to prolong it. Trying to be proactive, I shut the door. She cranks the engine, and I can't hold back a chuckle when she rolls down the window.

One last kiss, I think to myself. She's already in the

car, so surely it's safe enough. Leaning in, I take her lips again, losing myself in the warm softness of her mouth. I stop the kiss just before I yank the door open and pull her out of the car, and instead nod my head in the direction of the street.

She smiles at me, and I wink back at her. And then she's driving away, her taillights growing smaller as she makes her way toward home.

Something in me feels open, exposed, in a way it never has before. It's like I've shown her parts of myself that I've kept hidden all my life. My mind tells me I should be scared, but I don't feel the first thread of fear. All my life I've felt hollow inside, but not anymore. Rachelle has just jumped right in the middle of my heart and started digging around, finding every little empty space that existed in there and filling it up with *her*.

Chapter 17

GABE

RACHELLE IS PULLING the lasagna from the oven when I hear a knock on Ugly Mug's front door. Occasionally, on we're open during typical brunch hours on Sunday. It's a pretty short, calm day for whoever works those shifts. But since it's a holiday weekend, the place is closed, and Rachelle and I are cooking lunch for our moms.

"I got it." I lean over and kiss her cheek as she sets the lasagna on the counter, the cheesy aroma drifting up and filling the room.

Stepping out into the dining room, I see my mom at the door and can't help but smile. We've been through a lot, sacrificed more than anyone realizes for the life we have now, but the last four years together in Flagstaff have been completely worth it.

"Hey Mom." I greet her with a hug, and then take the chocolate cake from her hands. "Thanks for bringing dessert."

"I can't wait to meet her, Gabe," she whispers. The smile on her face tells me just how happy she is that I have a woman in my life.

"I haven't told her about Kansas City yet," I remind her. She knows this, of course. I just want to be sure she doesn't accidentally spill it. Not that my father and Sylvia are frequent topics of conversation, but still.

"So you've told me," Mom whispers. "If she's as special as you keep saying, it won't matter to her at all."

"I know that, Mom." I keep my voice down, just in case Rachelle comes out of the kitchen. "It's just a lot to throw at a girl this early in the relationship."

Mom rolls her eyes and nods, just as Rachelle emerges into the dining room. She looks nervous – I can tell by the way she clasps her hands in front of her and takes a deep breath. The tiny, silver studs in both her piercings catch the light as she approaches. She'd asked me if she should remove them altogether, but I'd just pointed at my gauged ears and told her my mom wouldn't bat an eye. She has absolutely nothing to worry about, but she's so darn cute all worked up over meeting my mom.

"Mom, this is Rachelle Taya." I look at Mom, then at Rachelle, struck at once that I'm standing between the two most important women in my life. "Rach, this is my mom, Andrea Williams."

"It's nice to meet you Ms. Williams," Rachelle says, reaching out to shake Mom's hand.

"Call me Andrea." Mom bypasses the hand and goes in for a hug. "I'm so glad to meet you. Gabe has told me so much about you."

Just then, the door opens again, and a woman who

could be no one besides Rachelle's mom steps in. It's like looking at a version of Rachelle in twenty years. Her mom is beautiful, just like she is, with dark ebony hair and bronze skin. She's a bit shorter than Rach, but her smile is the same. She seems more than a little nervous, and I want to put her at ease.

"I'm Gabe," I say, meeting her halfway between the door and where Mom and Rach are standing. "You must be Rachelle's mother."

She nods. "Jennifer Taya. It's good to meet you."

Taking a cue from my mom, I skip the handshake and go for the hug. At first she's startled, but it only takes a second for her to hug me back.

"I'm so glad to meet you, too."

Rachelle and my mom step up to us, and the expression in Rach's eyes tells me that she's grateful to me for making her mom feel welcome. She takes care of introducing the two moms, and I take a moment to appreciate what an awesome moment this is. It has to mean something that we're meeting each other's mothers, and that the moms are meeting each other. Like everything else with Rachelle, I want it to mean something.

"Can we help you get lunch ready?" Mom asks.

"We just got the lasagna out of the oven," I say, stepping over to lock the front door. "All that's left is to put the salad together and set the table."

Mom looks at Jennifer. "Why don't we take care of the salad while the two of them get the table ready?"

Jennifer seems pleased, as if being included wasn't something she expected. "All right. I can get the bread sliced as well," she replies, gesturing to her tote bag.

Our moms head off to the kitchen, and I slide my palm against Rachelle's and lace our fingers together. Her hand squeezes mine, and I swear I feel it in the center of my chest.

"So far, so good," she whispers.

"Yep," I say with a smile. Tugging her hand, but refusing to let go, I add, "I'll go grab the plates from the kitchen. You want to get the vase of flowers from upstairs?"

"Sounds like a plan."

Without releasing our hands, we make our way to the back of the dining room where I have a table for four waiting. Rachelle kisses my cheek and heads upstairs to get the flowers while I slip into the kitchen.

My mom's slicing cucumbers at one end of the kitchen, and Jennifer is at the sink rinsing lettuce. I wink at Mom then step quietly over to Jennifer.

"I'm really glad you're here." I lower my voice, hoping to convey the seriousness of what I'm about to say. I want her to know that her daughter is important to me. More important than anything has ever been. "Rachelle is very special to me. She's a wonderful woman, and I want you to know that I'm completely aware of that."

Jennifer smiles and nods her approval. She doesn't say anything, but she doesn't have to. The look in her eyes tells me she understands.

Before long, we're seated at the table with plates full of food. The conversation flows easily, and both moms seem content with the fact that their children are involved. It's not the traditional Labor Day barbecue, but I think the lasagna and salad helped us through our first major milestone as a couple.

Now, we just have to tackle the guys at Resolution.

Chapter 18

RACHELLE

"I 'VE MISSED YOU." Gabe's voice is nothing more than a husky growl as he leans in and crushes his mouth to mine. Completely unprepared for the sudden onslaught in the back parking lot of Resolution Ink, it takes me half a second to catch up.

But I do catch up.

Kissing Gabe is like visiting a museum and seeing the most beautiful piece of artwork you could ever imagine, while the most romantic and breathtaking music plays around you. His skin is slightly rough with a couple days' growth of beard, and I love the way it feels against my palms... and my cheeks.

I told him earlier in the week that stubble was sexy, so apparently he's skipped the razor the last few days.

Lunch with our moms turned out great, and the success of that event seems to have launched us from two people hanging out and exploring the possibilities to two people who can't get enough of each other. I can't decide if I'm elated or frightened, but I figure the fact that I've practically superglued my face to his says something.

He wraps his arms around me, sliding his hands beneath my jacket and pulling me closer while he kisses his way to my ear. Reaching for his waist, I grab onto his belt loops and hang on in order to keep my balance.

Kissing Gabe makes me dizzy. I figure that also says something about what's going on in my head and heart.

"You saw me this morning when I came in for coffee," I say, nuzzling against his neck. We've managed to at least lay eyes on each other every day since Labor Day, and one night he'd even picked up pizza and hung out with Mom and me at home. Tonight, we had no plans other than meeting up after work and grabbing some dinner.

"Yeah, but I couldn't do this in the middle of Ugly Mug."

And before I know it, I'm swallowed up again in the tidal wave of Gabe's kiss. One of his hands tangles in my hair, and I'm just about to do the same to him when the clanging of the back door and loud voices spilling out into the parking lot makes us jump apart.

Asher, Shane, Caleb, and Bing all stand there, mouths hanging open, saying absolutely nothing.

I look at Gabe. He takes a deep breath and winks, as if to tell me he's got this, before taking my hand.

"Hey guys," he says.

Shane steps up. "We're all headed out to for wings. Asher's picking up Grace on the way, and some girl Caleb knows is meeting us there. You two want to join us, or do you have something else planned?" He wiggles his eyebrows and delivers that last line with as much suggestion as possible.

Leave it to Shane to turn an awkward situation into something comical.

"Um…" I begin, congratulating myself on the brilliance of my vocabulary. I tell myself to just spit it out. "Gabe and I have been seeing each other."

Bing narrows his eyes, crossing his arms over his chest. Of all of them, he's the one I worry about the most. He's always seemed to like Gabe, but Brett Channing could certainly be over-protective when he decided to.

"You don't say?" Shane chuckles.

"For a few weeks," Gabe says, taking over the conversation. "Would've been longer if I'd worked up the nerve a little sooner."

"About time," Bing's voice rings out. A smile breaks out on his face, and I breathe a sigh of relief. "I was beginning to think you didn't have the balls."

Then the guys are shaking hands and slapping each other on the back, congratulating Gabe and me in the good-natured way that only friends can get away with. And these are my friends… the closest ones I've ever had. Maybe it's strange that my best friends are a rag tag group of tattoo artists, each with their own history and quirks, but it's the truth. Asher, Shane, and Caleb are some of the best men I know, and even though I didn't need their thumbs up to continue to spend time with Gabe, their approval pleases me immensely.

And then there's Bing. Our relationship goes much deeper than anyone realizes, going back all the way to when he saved me from becoming another statistic, another girl with no confidence, no plans, and no decent future. He, more than anyone else, knows why I've shied away from relationships, why I've always been skeptical when it comes to men and relationships. So to see the approval in his eyes means a great deal.

"I'm really happy for you, Rach," he whispers, wrapping me up in a hug. His arms tighten around me in a way that's always made me feel safe and important. "He's a good guy. A really good guy."

"I know." I nod and swallow past the lump in my throat. "Thank you, Brett."

Shane interrupts the moment, and I'm glad. I was seconds away from tears of happiness, which would've been embarrassing.

"We doing wings or what?" he says. "I'm tired of this hug fest."

Laughing, we pile into our cars and head out. My chest expands with a strange sensation I've never felt before. I don't examine it too closely, but I'm sure of one thing.

My heart is full.

Chapter 19

RACHELLE

I T'S MONDAY. NORMALLY, I greatly dislike Mondays, but today has been a good day. Work was smooth and easy. Gabe stopped by to bring me coffee mid-afternoon. Grace invited me on a shopping trip to Phoenix next week. Plus, I was just in a good mood. So yeah, today has been a good day.

As I'm driving home after work, it occurs to me that all my days have been good lately. My steps have been lighter. My smiles have been more frequent. I even made cupcakes one day and brought them to the guys at the shop. Bing grinned kind of suspiciously, but Caleb, Shane, and Asher just dug right in.

I know what Bing knew that day. My string of good days and happiness is because of Gabe.

We'd settled into a comfortable pattern over the last couple of weeks. I hit the coffee shop every morning before work, and he carves out a few minutes to sit down with me, even on mornings he doesn't have to work. He stops in at Resolution a few times a week and brings me lunch or an afternoon coffee, depending on his work schedule. Once a week he comes over to my place to have dinner with Mom and me. On weekends, we spend together as much as possible.

Mom's cool with the way things are. I think she's glad to see me happy and involved with someone as great as Gabe. She seems to occupy herself most of the time, and I don't feel so guilty about spending time with Gabe while she's at home. I hope her contentment means whatever financial problems she's dealing with are getting better.

I pull into the driveway of my little duplex and put the car in park. The lights are on in both sides of the house, indicating that Mr. Grainger, my landlord, is home. He's a single man in his late forties. I don't know if he's ever been married, but he's been single ever since I moved in. He's a nice man who always seems a little lonely. Maybe the next time Gabe comes for dinner, we'll invite him over.

As I'm unlocking the door, I hear Mom talking to someone on the phone. Pushing open the door, I see her at the kitchen table, and she's clearly not happy. I hear her say something about needing a payment plan and wanting to negotiate the interest rate. An open envelope and a few papers lay in front of her on the table, and I realize she must be attempting to deal with her financial situation.

I close the door quietly, trying not to disturb her, and hoping she will fill me in on the specifics so I can try to help. Not that I'm an expert, but sometimes having another perspective is beneficial.

But when she sees me, she wraps up the call immediately, telling whoever is on the other end that she'll call back and then shoves all the papers into her purse.

"You okay, Mom?" I ask. She looks a little shell-shocked, and I begin to worry that maybe this is more serious than a few overdue bills.

She nods, but looks away quickly. I pull out a chair and sit down at the table with her.

"Mom, you're obviously upset," I say, reaching for her hand. "Talk to me, please."

When she turns to face me, I see the tears spilling down her cheeks. My heart seizes, and for a moment I wonder if this has anything to do with money. What if something is really wrong, like with her health?

"I thought I had it under control," she whispers between breaths, trying to get control of the tears. "The money problems were significant, but not insurmountable. I just needed a year or so and I could've gotten out from under it all, but now..."

She stops mid-sentence and drops her head in her hands. I'm no genius with money, but I manage the books at Resolution, so I understand a bit about budgets and expenses and all that. Maybe I have something I can offer.

"Mom, will you please tell me what's going on," I plead. "What sort of problems are you having, and how bad are they?"

"I don't even know where to start," she says, not lifting her head.

"Just start at the beginning."

She sits up straight and takes a deep breath, as if shoring herself up for the conversation. Regardless of the fact that she's somehow managed to land in some sticky financial mess, my mom is the strongest person I've ever known. Given all the obstacles she's had to overcome – a less than stellar upbringing, an abusive marriage, no formal education or skills training – the fact that she'd been able to get us out of that awful situation, raise me on her own, and support herself is more than admirable.

"It started out with a credit card bill a couple of years ago." She closes her eyes. "It was maxed out at around five thousand dollars."

Shit. I bite my tongue to keep from saying it out loud, and remind myself that lots of people find themselves in this situation every day. "You're not the first person to get into credit card trouble."

Mom nods. "At first, I was making payments, trying to get the balance down. But when you can only pay the minimum due, it doesn't make a lot of difference. Then the interest went up, and I couldn't even make the minimum payments."

"Couldn't you work out some kind of payment plan?" I ask. To my knowledge we hadn't had a credit card while I was growing up, so maybe Mom didn't even know what resources she had.

"I probably should've tried, but…" she chokes on a sob again. A moment later she continues. "I did something stupid. I missed a few payments because I just couldn't make ends meet. When the collection agency started calling, I changed my cell phone number."

With that, the tears begin all over again. She's right. That was an incredibly stupid move. But I remember enough from my childhood to know what it feels like to be desperate financially, so I can't be mad. I'm just so sorry she's found herself in this predicament in the first place.

"I'm not proud of it." She wipes at her eyes, taking a deep breath. "I just didn't want to think about it anymore."

"Mom," I say gently, taking her hand again. "How did you manage to run up five thousand dollars worth of credit card debt?"

"It was your father's card," she answers. "He'd taken it out some time previously, but both our names were on the account. When he stopped paying the interest started building up, and when they finally found me, it was just out of control."

I can literally feel my blood pressure rising, the pulse in my temples throbbing with anger. I'm furious that he's a part of this. He's been gone for ten years, and his bullshit is still causing my mom problems.

"So, this is some kind of leftover debt from when you were married?" I ask. Not that it's hard to believe. The notion that my dad would've taken out a credit card in both their names, without telling Mom, and then maxed it out and bailed on paying the bill is not surprising.

Mom just nods. "Eventually, the collection agency found me, but by that time, they'd already started court proceedings. There was a judgment against me, and they started garnishing my paychecks. For a few months I managed, but then it just became too much. I couldn't pay my rent and other bills with what was leftover after they took their cut."

I swallow hard, counting backwards from ten trying to get my temper under control. Disbelief sears through me at the thought that my lousy father can still be screwing us over even after he's been gone for ten years. I'm also having a hard time with the fact that Mom kept me in the dark for so long.

"Why didn't you tell me sooner?" I ask. "Before this got so out of hand?"

"I didn't want you to have to deal with any of this." She wipes the wetness from her cheeks, trying to get her composure back. "I'm the parent. You're the child. You're not supposed to have to worry about my financial situation."

"You and I have been a team for a long time, Mom. It's time to let me help, even if all I can do is be shoulder to cry on sometimes."

"Okay," she whispers.

"Now you've got to tell me what that phone call was about." I scoot my chair closer to hers so she can't avoid looking at me. "You said you thought you had it handled, but something changed that."

"I got another bill in the mail." Her voice is soft, her

tone defeated. "Another credit card, which is also maxed out. He hasn't made payments in a long time. When the first company got that judgment against me, I guess it made it easier for this one to find me. God knows they can't find him."

"Can I see it?" I gesture to her purse, where she stuffed the papers when I came in.

She sighs in resignation and hands the papers to me. My stomach drops when I see that she's right. This one is just as bad as the one she described already. A look at the envelope tells me that she's still getting her mail at the post office. That was a precaution she took when we moved into our first place after my dad left. We didn't want him to be able to easily track us down. It's also a practice I've adopted. No sense giving him a way to find me.

"I just don't understand how they can hold you solely responsible for this." I shuffle through the papers as if something in the fine print will suddenly jump out at me with an answer. Then I catch a glimpse of the most recent charges. They were made ten months ago. No way should she still be responsible for those. I was young when the two of them split, and I know she probably shielded me from the hassle of the divorce, but she can't be made to pay for the shit he's done since then. "There has to be some way that we can at least get them to back off the charges he's made since you all divorced."

Mom slams her eyes shut and drops her head into her hands again and says nothing.

"You have told them you're not married to him anymore, haven't you?" I ask.

She says nothing, just keeps her head down.

Her shoulders begin to shake, and I can see that she's crying again.

"Mom?" I whisper, a feeling of dread unfurling in the pit of my stomach as possibilities for her reaction to my question begin to take shape in my mind. "Why haven't you told them that?"

She raises her head, red-rimmed tear-filled eyes finding mine. Whatever she's about to tell me, she's resigned herself to it, as if once she says it something between us will change irrevocably.

"Because legally we're still married." Shame fills her voice as nausea rolls through my gut. "I never divorced him."

Chapter 20

GABE

I'M ALWAYS AMAZED at the volume of mail we get at Ugly Mug. Most of it's junk, so it just requires a bit of sorting to pull out the bills and important stuff then dump the rest in the garbage. Dropping it all on the island, I grab the pretzels from the counter and reach in the fridge for a root beer.

I've noticed that Rachelle always seems surprised to look in my refrigerator and not see beer. Not that she's said anything, but I can tell she wonders why I'm not like most twenty-two year old guys with nothing but beer, mustard, and old pizza. I know I should tell her why. Not because she needs an explanation about my beverage choices, but because it relates directly to my past and the people I used to call my family. That, of course, kind of affects my relationship with her because of the things we have in common.

Which she has no idea about since I haven't told her.

I'm such a douche.

I don't really know what I'm worried about. Rachelle isn't judgmental, and I've never known her to behave irrationally. But somehow, telling her that I watched my dad get drunk and beat the shit out of my mom for years and years makes my insides turn to ice. Not to mention that domestic violence isn't the worst thing on my dad's resume of bad deeds.

I toss three catalogs of restaurant supply items into the trash, and my heart stops when I see the return address of the letter underneath.

Sylvia Barlow Jenkins.

My brain screams at me to drop Sylvia's envelope in the trash on top of the catalogs... to just throw it in there, unopened and unread. I'm not sure if it's stupidity or morbid curiosity that has me ripping open the flap and pulling out the contents.

Immediately I notice that in addition to her letter is some sort of newspaper article. Ignoring the clipping, I read Sylvia's unusually short note.

Gabriel,

I thought you might be interested in your father's recent accomplishment. While it may be difficult to believe, he is making great strides in atoning for his past behavior. I hope you'll take a moment to read and perhaps consider a trip home in the near future.

Bile burns the back of my throat. Looking at what she's sent me is the last thing I want to do, but I can't stop myself. With shaking hands, I unfold the article and scan my eyes over it.

First, I notice the picture. My father, in standard

prison clothes, along with a few others, removing some kind of wood and debris from the front lawn of a concrete building. Second, I read the headline: *Local Prison Suffers Damage in Recent Storm.*

The article goes on to detail how high winds damaged several buildings on the prison grounds – thankfully, not the ones that house prisoners. Apparently, the reception center and one of the storage units lost their roofs and metal siding. My dad isn't listed by name, but a number of prisoners apparently worked on the clean-up detail, which the article says points to the success of the prison system helping inmates get their shit together and clean up their acts.

I close the bag of pretzels and stick the root beer back in the refrigerator, unopened. I'm just about to wad Sylvia's letter and the article into the trash, when a text alert beeps from my phone.

When I see it's from Rachelle, I push all thoughts of Sylvia and my father to the back of my mind, grab my phone, and settle on the couch to text with my girl.

> **Rachelle:** *My Monday has sucked. Wish we'd made plans to see each other tonight.*
>
> **Me:** *My night is total crap. Work was hectic and having coffee with you this morning wasn't enough. Wanna sneak over here?*
>
> **Rachelle:** *Tempting, but I can't. In the middle of laundry, which is the perfect end to a fantastic day. Insert sarcastic eye roll here.*
>
> **Gabe:** *Coffee in the morning? The scones you like are*

on the menu.

Rachelle: *You know I'll be there, scones or not. :)*

Gabe: *I miss you.*

Rachelle: *Same.*

I want to tell her a whole lot more than that I miss her, but I know it's too soon. I settle for a bit of truth that points toward what I'm really feeling for her.

Gabe: *This thing with us? It's a big deal to me, Rach. I want you to know that.*

Rachelle: *I know, Gabe. It is for me, too.*

Gabe: *Just so we're clear, I'm not letting you go.*

Rachelle: *I sure as hell hope not.*

Chapter 21

RACHELLE

THE LAST APPOINTMENTS for the day are finally gone. Shane and Caleb are straightening their stations in preparation for tomorrow, and Asher left twenty minutes ago to meet Grace for dinner. I've been in a nasty mood all day, and I'm sure they all noticed. This morning over coffee, Gabe kept asking if I was okay. I evaded him. At work, Shane inquired a couple of times what was wrong, but after I snapped his head off, he stopped asking.

I hate that I've been mean to him and snippy with everyone else. But what I hate worse is the reason my disposition sucks so bad.

All day I've gone back and forth between total numbness and consuming anger. The anger I get. It feels good, even… like I've tapped into the kind of emotion that I'm supposed to be feeling. But then, for long moments, I feel nothing. Just an emptiness that threatens to swallow me.

That's the feeling that scares me.

And it's made a bitch all day long.

Shane and Caleb had talked incessantly about the

Assassin's Creed marathon they had planned, complete with pizza and Chinese take-out because they couldn't agree on what kind of food to order. Asher and Grace were going out to dinner and then back to her apartment to catch up on some TV series they had DVRed.

I'm going home to Mom. Mom, who is still married to the man who beat her up on a regular basis and did little more than donate sperm so I could exist. I hate that he's connected to me at all.

And along with the discontent that thought brings comes the guilt. Guilt because she's my mom. She worked herself to the bone before and after Dad left so that I could have what I needed. We never had a lot, but we never went without, and that was all because of her. It shouldn't rankle me so much that she needs my help now. Lord knows she's earned it.

I can't believe she did all that but failed to divorce him.

And I just miss the kind of relationship we developed once I became an adult and moved out on my own. Now, with the two of us under the same roof again, it's like we're back to being teenager and overprotective mom. Not that she gives me a curfew or tries to keep tabs on me or anything. But I miss being able to just leave my apartment or stay out late without having to explain.

I'm finishing up a supply order when Bing opens the door to the small office just off the lobby.

"Rach, can you come in here for a minute?" he asks.

"Sure. Just let me submit this order."

I click to complete the order, print the confirmation, and head across to the office.

"Go ahead and have a seat," Bing says.

"Am I fired?" I ask, joking as he closes his laptop. Brett Channing, or Bing as he's known to practically everyone, looks, to the rest of the world, like a hard ass, but in reality he has a heart as big as the Grand Canyon.

"Of course not," he laughs.

"We're out!" Shane calls from the lobby.

"All right," Bing says. "We'll lock up."

He listens for the back door to close, signaling that Shane and Caleb have left, then leans across the desk toward me.

"So what's with the foul attitude today?"

Bing never minces words.

I sigh. I know I need to tell him, but it's just so freaking embarrassing. I know it's stupid, but I just don't want to say the words out loud.

"It's Mom," I say simply, hoping maybe that will be enough.

"I know the situation's stressful, but it's not new. Today's bitchiness, on the other hand, *is* new."

I drop my head, my jaw tightening and my foot tapping. There's no use trying to evade him. "Bing, it's so much worse than I thought. So much worse than she led me to believe."

"How much worse?" he asks in that quiet, confident way he has, like he's certain he'll have the answer to my problems. Even though I'm certain he won't.

"I walked in yesterday and she was on the phone with a credit card company. I could tell she'd been crying. She shoved the papers in her purse and tried to act like nothing was wrong, but I forced her to be straight with me about where these money problems originated," I begin, still not looking him in the eye. "It's not just fewer hours and more expensive rent. It's that foul excuse for a father."

Bing raises his eyebrows, malice creeping into his expression.

"They never got divorced," I whisper, ringing my hands. The admission is painful and humiliating. "They're still legally married."

"What the hell?" he asks, but I know he doesn't expect an answer.

"When she kicked him out, she was just so glad to be rid of him, so glad he stayed gone. For the first year or so, we were so afraid he'd come back. She worked extra hours to save enough so we could move out of that trailer. She even rented a post office box so there wouldn't be a physical address under her name." I stopped to take a breath. Bing didn't say anything – he just waited patiently for me to go on. "I was just eleven when he left, so I just assumed that meant their marriage was over and they'd get divorced. She thought eventually they'd go through with a divorce, but then he disappeared and she didn't have the money to pursue it anyway. So she just forgot about it. Or ignored it. So the two of them are still legally married, and now Dad has run up a mountain of credit card debt in both their names that she's partially responsible for. The creditors can't find him, so they've come after her. They've garnished her wages. Her credit is shot to shit. And when she finally showed me the bills and I got a look at the balances, I don't know how she's ever going to pay it all off."

"Wow," Bing says, shaking his head. "That's heavy."

"I don't even know where to start, Bing. I guess we need a lawyer because we need someone to walk us through this, tell us what options we have, if we even have any. But I don't know how either of us is going to afford it."

Bing runs a hand across his buzzed head. "I've done some work for a lawyer in town. I can make a phone call and see what help there is. There'd probably still be some cost involved, but maybe we could work something out. I can help, too."

"I hate asking for help."

Bing is not surprised by that statement. "I know. But you didn't ask. I offered. And it sounds like your mom is out of options."

I nod, knowing he's right. "We don't just need the money problems resolved. Mom has got to finally divorce him."

Just the thought that their marriage is still legally binding makes my blood boil. I've got to do something with all this nervous energy, so I push to my feet, turning to pace the floor.

"I know that," Bing says, coming around from behind his desk and perching on the corner. He grabs my hand to stop my movement. "Part of your mom's problem is that she tried to deal with this on her own. I get it. No one wants to admit this kind of thing to their family. But she's not alone anymore. She's got you on her side, and me as well. We'll find a way to get through it."

"Thank you," I whisper, putting my arms around him. Resting my head on his shoulder, I take a deep breath.

And notice Gabe standing just outside the open office door.

"I didn't mean to interrupt." His expression is almost blank, but I can see the thread of hurt just beneath the surface.

"You're not interrupting, Gabe," I say, stepping out of the office. He takes a step back from me, and my heart sinks.

"I know we didn't have plans tonight, but I cut out early from the shop and thought I'd see if you wanted to grab some dinner with me, but you've obviously got a lot to deal with, so I'll head out." He backs up another step. "Another time."

Gabe slips out the front door, and I feel lower than gum on the bottom of a shoe. The sweet connection that had been forming between us now feels frayed to the point of breaking, and it's entirely my fault. He'd been so careful not to push me for information, but so conscientious to give me opportunities to share. Why hadn't I shared everything with him?

Bing steps out of the office and drapes an arm around my shoulder. "Go to him, Rachelle. He's a good guy. A little crazy, but decent through and through. You need to tell him everything. You can't keep this all bottled up and telling me isn't going to allow you to let go of it. You have to let him in. He'll understand and be supportive.

I swallow hard and nod.

"I'll let your mom know where you are."

Grabbing my purse, I practically sprint through the shop and out the back door to my car.

Chapter 22

GABE

I KNOW IT'S her as soon as I hear the knock.

Once upon a time, I might've been the shitty guy who didn't answer the door. But I don't even hesitate tonight. I open it immediately.

Rachelle stands on the other side, bottom lip caught between her teeth and an uneasy expression on her face. Not that I'd been mad at her before, but if I had been, seeing her all cute and worried would be enough to stem the anger.

"Hey," I say, stepping back to give her room. "Come on in."

She keeps a few feet between us, like she's expecting me to lash out and is surprised that I'm not. I hate the uncertainty in her eyes. Hate that she's too skittish to get close to me.

I'm not exactly sure what I'm supposed to say, so I just wait for her.

"Please don't be mad," she whispers.

"I'm not mad." I turn and walk to the kitchen. If she needs distance between us, I can accommodate. The last thing I want is for her to be afraid of me.

Needing something to busy myself with, I fill two glasses with ice and grab a root beer from the fridge. "Just confused."

"Confused?" she asks. She follows me to the kitchen and leans against the island.

"I thought things were going great between us." I pour one glass, then the second, and slide it across toward her. "I wanted you to confide in me, and I was doing my best to build trust so you'd tell me when you were ready. Just kind of stings that you couldn't talk to me."

"Gabe," she whispers, not touching the glass.

"But I get it." I drain half my glass and set it down a bit harder than necessary. I know I'm being all kinds of hypocritical given that there's quite a bit I haven't told her about myself, but at least my secrets are long past, not the immediate present. "You've known Bing a long time. I know you trust him. But I'm your boyfriend, and I just kind of wanted you to trust me, too."

"You're my boyfriend?" she asks, her eyes wide.

"Maybe it sounds high-schoolish, but yeah. That's how I think of our relationship. And we *are* in a relationship. I don't want anybody else, and I don't want you to want anybody else, so that means I'm your boyfriend. And I get it if you don't want that label right now, but I can't help that I feel that way."

"*Boyfriend*," she repeats, her eyes no longer wary, but filled with laughter.

A smile tugs at the corner of my mouth, but I hold it back, not exactly sure where she's going with this. I cross my arms across my chest and just wait.

"I love that word," she whispers, closing the distance until she's right in front of me sliding her hands up my arms. "I want to be your girl, Gabe."

I don't hesitate. Don't wait to see if she has something else to say. As soon as the words leave her mouth, I take her face between my palms and seal my lips to hers. She opens immediately, welcoming me with her warmth as I all but devour her. Her hands slide from my biceps to my chest, and I crush her closer. My mind is racing, trying unsuccessfully to keep up with my heart as it falls further and further into her. Somewhere in the back of my mind, I know there's no coming back from this. She's it for me.

She pulls back and smiles up at me, her eyes glazed with the effects of our kiss. I could look at her forever. Seriously.

"I trust you," she says, certainty lacing the soft whisper of her voice. "Please know that. It wasn't lack of trust that kept me from confiding in you. It was shame."

"Shame?" I slide my arms around her waist and pull her flush against me.

"That my mom, who in so many ways is an amazing woman, could've been so stupid about my father."

"That's not your fault." I tighten my hold on her. "You know that, right?"

She nods. "I didn't choose to talk to Bing *instead* of

you. I talked to him because he's my brother."

I've known the crew at Resolution – including Bing and Rachelle – for over two years. Never once did anyone mention that the two of them are related. The shock I feel must show on my face because she launches into an explanation immediately.

"He's my half-brother," she begins. "We didn't grow up together. In fact, I didn't even know about him until I was fifteen. We have the same dad, although he's a sorry excuse for a father."

"Let's sit." I pick up our glasses and nod toward the couch. I'm dying to ask all sorts of questions, like how come I never knew the two of them were related, but I figure she's got to tell me at her own speed. "May as well be comfortable."

Rachelle smiles and follows me. She settles into one corner of the sofa as I sit our glasses on the coffee table. I take the end opposite her and pull her feet into my lap. She looks at me funny when I slip one of her sandals off.

"Keep talking," I say with a wink, tossing the second sandal to the floor, noticing that her leggings have a pattern of pink hearts and orange smiley faces. Her wardrobe makes me smile. "Don't mind me."

"Bing's mom got pregnant in high school," she says. "They didn't get married, which was a blessing, because then Bing's childhood would've been just like mine."

Anger wells in my gut at the thought of what that statement could mean. I don't ask, though, because I figure she'll get to it eventually. Instead, I ask about something less painful.

"That's why you have different last names?"

She nods. "His mom's name was Ava Channing. She eventually got married to his stepdad, Paul Stewart, and Bing never really knew his biological father, although eventually his mom told him *about* his father. And by the way, Bing's first name is actually Brett."

"No kidding?" Her feet now bare, I pull them both into my lap. I wrap my hands around them and begin running my thumb along her instep.

"What are you doing?" she asks, looking at me like I've grown second head on my shoulders.

"Foot massage. Hasn't anyone ever rubbed your feet?'

She shakes her head, and I smile. I'm secretly elated that I'm the first to do this for her.

"You talk," I say, adding a little more pressure with my thumbs. "I rub your feet."

"I'm not sure I can talk while you do that." Her eyes close, and her voice sounds fuzzy.

"What if I ask a few questions?" I ask, moving my efforts to the backs of her heels.

She nods. "As long as you keep doing that."

I smile, thinking maybe I've found a way into her heart.

"How come no one talks about the fact that you and Bing are siblings?"

"No one knows," she says. "As soon as I turned eighteen, he gave me a job in the shop. At first it was just answering phones and greeting people. I was good at it, and pretty soon he started giving me more responsibility. He showed me how to keep the books and added my name to the business account so I could write checks and pay bills. There was a lot of turnover at first, other than Caleb, guys didn't stay all that long before moving on to other shops or bigger cities, so we never really got close enough to share it with any of them. But Caleb stuck around, and once Shane landed, and Asher not long after, I didn't want them to think I was getting special treatment, so I asked him not to tell them."

"You've been there three years, Rach," I say, gently massaging the pads of her toes. "Surely by now they know you've earned your place. Why not tell them?"

She shrugs. "Bringing up our connection means bringing up our father, and that's a subject neither of us is in a hurry to talk about. He's an asshole."

"I can understand that." Not wanting to talk about an asshole father is a concept I'm intimately familiar with. "I'm glad you told me."

"I guess you heard that Bing's going to call a lawyer he knows." She lays her head back on the arm of the couch and sighs, heavy and deep. "Although even if Bing can get a favor, it'll still cost money that I don't have and Mom sure doesn't have."

"Yeah, I heard." In my head I'm already formulating a plan. I need to get the name of that attorney without raising anyone's suspicions. "I'm sure there's something that can be done to help."

Rachelle closes her eyes and lets out a heavy sigh. "I

hope so, Gabe."

"Rach," I say, sliding my palm gently across her lower leg. When she looks up at me, I go on. "Why was your dad such an asshole?"

"My dad is Hopi. We're not sure about Mom. She was adopted and never knew her birth parents. She looks like a mix of Native and Anglo. We didn't live on a reservation, but we did live in a trailer park full of other dirt poor Hopi people." She takes a deep breath and leans her head back on the arm of the couch. "He beat my mom. Regularly. My family fell into the cycle of domestic violence that's prevalent in so many Native American communities."

I had a feeling it was something like that, but hearing it confirmed rips me up inside.

"Did he hit you?"

She shakes her head. "No. But he wasn't discreet with his violence toward Mom, so I watched it all happen. I think in a way that's worse than getting beat up myself."

I'm not so sure about that, but watching your dad treat your mom like a punching bag is no way to spend your childhood. I should know. Somewhere in the back of my mind I know I should tell her the truth, let her know I can relate, but I convince myself it can wait. Relief that Rachelle wasn't physically hurt courses through me like an avalanche, so I concentrate on that.

"How old were you when they split up?"

"Eleven," she answers, lifting her head to look up at

me. "It's been ten years, and she's still married to that piece of shit."

"We'll figure out a way to fix that," I say, grasping her hands and pulling her up and into my arms. I slide one hand into the mass of ebony hair at the back of her neck and press a kiss to her forehead. "And we'll find a way to solve the money problems, too."

She pulls back enough to look at me and narrows her eyes. "We?"

"You don't think I'm letting you go through this alone, do you?" I press my palm against the side of her face, my thumb tracing lightly across her cheek. "I'm here."

She tilts her head, warmth spreading across her expression and moisture glistening in her eyes. Her lips meet mine, not with passion or excitement, but with an emotion so intense I can't describe it.

"Thank you," she whispers, her mouth still resting against mine. "So much. I've been so miserable all day. Numb and angry and closed-off. But I can't be that way with you."

I'm gone. I'm so far gone, and I don't even care. I'd walk through the fires of hell for this woman and not think twice.

I'm in love with Rachelle Taya.

Chapter 23

GABE

RACHELLE IS GROCERY shopping this afternoon. I know this because over coffee this morning she announced she was cooking me dinner tonight. At my place. And yes, I'm thrilled that she feels comfortable just inviting herself over.

Her shift ended at three o'clock, and I'm pulling into Resolution's back parking lot fifteen minutes later. Her car is gone, so I know the coast is clear.

I shoot a text to Asher and ask him to let me in the back door, hoping he's not in the middle of inking a client. Lucky for me, he appears at the door a minute later.

"You ready to finalize that new design?" he asks, referring to the new tattoo we've been brainstorming.

"Still thinking on it," I say. "But I do want to sit down and talk about it again soon. I'm actually here to see Bing."

"Something to do with Rachelle?" Asher asks, walking beside me down the hall.

I nod and wink, hoping he'll continue with the notion that whatever I'm here for has more to do with romancing Rachelle instead of helping her and her mom out of a jam. Not that Ash or any of these guys would think less of her. In fact, I know they'd all do just about anything to help her out; but this is Rach's private life, and it's a sensitive matter, so sharing it with them is up to her.

Asher bumps my shoulder with his and disappears back into his work-room. I head up toward the front, knowing Bing is probably behind the counter since Rachelle is gone. He seems to approve of my relationship with his sister, so I hope he won't think twice about my asking questions.

Naturally, I'm not about to tell him about my trust fund or the fact that I can make all Rachelle's problems disappear, but I figure letting him know that I want to help can't hurt.

I turn into the lobby just as Bing hangs up the phone. No one is sitting in the waiting area, which means we're alone. Perfect.

"Gabe." Bing stands up to shake my hand. "Rachelle just left a few minutes ago."

I take a second to appreciate the fact that Rach and I are enough of an item that he just assumed I was here for her. I like that our relationship has melded smoothly into the lives of the people most important to us.

"Yeah, I know," I say. "I actually came by to talk to you."

Bing nods and gestures to his office door. "Let's talk

in my office. Less chance we'll be overheard, and I can still watch the front desk from in there."

He leaves the door open just a crack and twists the blinds on the window that looks out toward the lobby so the room is in full view. He doesn't sit down, but rather balances against the corner of his desk, so I follow suit and lean a shoulder on the door jam.

"I'm assuming she told you everything," he begins.

"She did." I pause for effect and add, "Brett."

He chuckles. "Rach still calls me that from time to time, but other than that, I've been Bing since I started in this line of work. Nicknames have a way of sticking around here."

"Maybe I'll nickname Asher and see how he likes it," I say, thankful for the fact that Bing and I can joke around. Dating a guy's sister can be a tricky thing. "Ashtray. Ashamed. Ash-hole."

"Let me know how those go over." Bing laughs again, before taking a deep breath. "You want to talk to me about Rachelle's predicament?"

"I want to help, if I can."

"I'm sure you do," he says. "And I'm glad you want to be there for Rachelle, but I don't know that any of us can do much of anything, short of letting the legal system take its course."

"She said you knew an attorney who might be able to give some advice?" I ask, keeping my voice neutral. I don't want Bing to know that I need the lawyer's name.

"I've done some work for her." Bing pushes away

from the desk to look out the window that faces the street. "She's actually on her way here now."

"Do you think she'll be able to help?"

"I'm sure she'll do what she can," he answers. "But I don't know if her firm will allow her to just do this for us pro-bono, and I wouldn't ask that anyway. I have a bit of money I can use to help out. Hopefully she'll have some ideas that we haven't thought of."

"I have a little money as well." A little is an understatement, but I'm not telling him that. "Living above Ugly Mug and not paying rent means I've been able to save some." Which is the truth, just not all of it. "Plus, running a business in town means you meet people and make connections. Maybe between you and me we know enough people to give us some help."

Bing's eyes shift to the front window where a tall, very attractive blonde in a navy blue skirt and jacket is heading toward the door. Instead of a purse, she carries a leather satchel.

"That's her," Bing says, stepping out into the lobby just as she opens the front door.

"Hello Brett." She doesn't see me at first, and I can't help but notice the tone of familiarity in her voice.

Brett. She called him *Brett.* Which, according to him, only Rachelle calls him, and even then it's only sometimes.

"Kristy, this is Gabe Jenkins." Bing motions to me. "He's a friend of the shop. Gabe, this is Kristy Fletcher."

"Nice to meet you," I say, reaching out to shake her

hand.

"You, as well," she replies.

I get the sense that the conversation about to take place between her and Bing is more private that I first thought, and since I want Bing to feel at ease confiding in her about Rachelle's problems, I decide to make myself scarce. Besides, now I know her name. It won't be much of a stretch to find out where she works.

"I've got to head back to work." I reach in my pocket for my Jeep keys. "Bing, we'll catch up later, okay?"

"Absolutely," he says.

"Again, nice to meet you, Ms. Fletcher."

"Just Kristy," she says. "No need to be formal."

Which tells me things aren't exactly formal between her and Bing.

With one last goodbye, I head down the hallway. I poke my head in Asher's door and say a quick *catch you later* to him, before making my way out back.

As I drive back toward Ugly Mug, I dial the number of the attorney who handled the transfer of my trust fund last year. I haven't needed to call him since the fund became mine, so I have no idea what to do to withdraw any of the funds.

I figure now is the time to find out.

Chapter 24

RACHELLE

GABE'S APARTMENT SMELLS fantastic. Homemade pizza topped with Italian sausage, peppers, onions, mushrooms, and plenty of cheese bakes and bubbles away in the oven, filling the room with a cheesy, garlicky aroma. A salad of mixed greens, kalamata olives, and feta cheese is ready to be tossed with the vinaigrette dressing I made earlier.

And on the island is a turtle cheesecake I ordered from my favorite bakery.

Gabe is finishing up some things downstairs at Ugly Mug, making sure everything is ready for the evening crowd. I've enjoyed these moments alone, cooking in his kitchen. The bit of domesticity has been a nice break from the seemingly insurmountable stress of my real life.

Mom and I have been iffy around one another since her big reveal. Her, because she's afraid I'm going to blow up at any second. Me, because I just don't know what to say. I have no answers, and I simply cannot fathom how she could let this go on for so long – the marriage and the money issues – without asking for help.

I understand pride, more so than most people, but even I can't figure out how she thought it was all going to go away if she ignored it.

This morning when I came into Ugly Mug for coffee, I decided that for tonight I just needed Gabe. So, here I am cooking dinner for the two of us.

"Something smells amazing!" I hear Gabe call out from the stairwell before he even turns the doorknob. When he steps into the apartment, he closes his eyes and breathes in deep. Eyes still closed, he goes on. "You're moving in, right? I can't ever let you leave because I want my apartment to always smell like this."

I can't help the giggle that bubbles in my chest. I wrap my arms around his waist and lay my head on his chest, happier than I can explain to be alone with him. His arms embrace me, his strength pouring into me, as he nuzzles his lips against my neck.

"I'm so glad you're here," he whispers.

"Me too."

"Is that a cheesecake?" he asks.

I nod.

"Now I'm certain I can't let you leave."

"If you want another cheesecake when that one's gone, you'll have to let me leave," I say. "I didn't make it. It came from a bakery."

"Cheater," he says with a chuckle, leaning down to press a kiss to my cheek. He grasps my hand and walks toward the kitchen. "Can I help get things ready?"

"You can take care of the drinks," I answer, peeking

in the oven to see that the pizza is perfect. I grab two oven mitts from the counter and prepare to take it out of the oven. "Root beer is fine, unless you'd rather have something stronger."

"I don't do stronger," Gabe says, shaking his head. "Unless you mean coffee."

Not that I think it's a flaw or anything, but I still can't help but wonder why I've never seen him drink alcohol or why there's never beer in his refrigerator.

"I see the questions on your face, Rach." He sits two cans of root beer on the counter. "I've just seen enough of what it can do to a person. I decided not to go down that path."

"Nothing wrong with that."

"But that doesn't mean we can't drink root beer out of fancy glasses," he says with a wink, opening the cabinet above the stove and pulling out two wine glasses. "Sometimes I even splurge on the expensive kind in glass bottles."

I smile, thinking about how nice it is that Gabe continues to surprise me. Opening the oven, I carefully remove the pizza, sitting it on the stovetop to cool.

"Homemade pizza?" Gabe's eyes nearly roll back in his head. "Are you sure you can't move in?"

I know he's only joking about moving in, but I can't help the little flutter that skips through me each time he mentions it. There's a secret part of me that wonders if the two of us are headed down the path that leads to commitment and forever and all that.

He reaches to pick a mushroom, and I slap his hand away. "It's got to cool off before we can slice it."

His fake pout is just about the cutest thing I've ever seen. Tip-toeing up, I kiss his frown away.

"Get some plates," I say, my lips still pressed against his. "And forks."

Once we're seated at the island, our barstools pulled side-by-side, conversation flows easily over salad and pizza. It's during the cheesecake course that Gabe brings up my mom.

"So, what's going on with your mom? Any movement on that front?" he asks.

"Not much." Sighing, I reach for my glass and take a drink. "Bing was supposed to be meeting with the attorney he knows sometime today. Hopefully he'll have something to tell me tomorrow."

Gabe nods. "I dropped by the shop this afternoon, just after you left. I wanted to let Bing know I'm here to help however I can. The lawyer showed up before I left."

"Did he look smart?" I ask. I haven't been able to decide if I want a lawyer who looks intelligent or ruthless.

"*She* looked very smart and professional," he replies. "But I only said hello, then left them to their conversation."

I see the speculation in Gabe's eyes. "Was *she* young and pretty?"

"Yes and yes," he says. "And she called him Brett."

I'm torn between worrying that the possible object of

Bing's affection might not be exactly what my mom needs and being giddy that my brother might have a woman in his life.

"He said he'd done some work for her." I put the last bite of cheesecake in my mouth and savor it before I go on. "Did you see any ink?"

Gabe shakes his head. "Nope. Which means he put it somewhere she can keep hidden."

"I can't believe we're sitting here pondering Bing's love life," I say with a laugh. "Correction. His *potential* love life."

"Especially when we've got such a smoking hot one ourselves." Gabe takes my hand and leads me over to the sofa.

And we spend the next hour making out like teenagers. I didn't have regular teenage experiences, and I'm getting the sense that maybe he didn't either, so making out on the couch seems like some sort of rite of passage we're just now getting around to.

That – and the fact that Gabe is an amazing kisser – makes this the perfect way to end the evening.

Chapter 25

GABE

THREE WEEKS AFTER homemade pizza night – and a whole host of other official dates and stolen moments – Rachelle walks into Ugly Mug on her way to work, per our normal routine.

But today something's different. I can tell in the sexy sway of her hips and the gleam in her eye as she approaches the counter that something has her in a better than usual mood. Not to mention that she looks drop dead gorgeous in that shade of pink, her long ebony hair hanging in soft waves down her back.

"Morning beautiful," I say, sliding the dirty chai toward her. She goes back and forth between coffee with hazelnut flavor and chai with a shot of espresso, so I've taken to just surprising her with one or the other every morning. It's always ready when she walks in the door, along with whatever scone is the freshest. It's a silly ritual, but I love it. I love that we have rituals, and I think she does, too.

"Hey Gabe." She leans across the counter and I meet her halfway, for a quick but sweet good morning kiss.

"Guess what?"

"I have absolutely no idea, but I can't wait for you to tell me."

She tilts her head toward an empty table. I give Harrison a shout to make sure he's got the counter covered and follow her over.

"So," she begins as soon as I'm seated, "the attorney, Kristy Fletcher, is going to be able to help us for a really small fee."

"Really?" I ask, keeping my expression indifferent. "That's great news."

Rachelle nods. "Apparently, from time to time there are funds available for the attorneys at her firm to do pro bono work. There will be some fees involved, but she's going to be able to waive a lot of it for us."

"That's got to be a relief." I pinch off a bite of her blueberry scone and pop it in my mouth. She pretends to be offended but then smiles. "Any details on what she thinks is the next step?"

"Probably bankruptcy," she says. "It'll get rid of a lot of the debt. She'll also start divorce proceedings once the financial plan is in place."

I hadn't asked Kristy for the details of her plan when I dropped off the check for her retainer. I didn't think it was my place to meddle in the process. I just want to make certain Rachelle's mom gets out of financial quicksand and finally manages to divorce the man who's abused her for far too long.

Of course, Rachelle and Bing have no idea I'm behind the pro bono part of the deal, or that Kristy, who I believe has true, deep feelings for Bing, is doing a lot of the work on her own time so she can keep even that cost down. I know they would both be reluctant to accept help from me, and I don't necessarily want to explain how it is I have so much money. That's a can of worms I've been hesitant to open.

I know I should. The longer I wait to tell Rachelle the truth about my father and the rest of my family, the harder it's going to be. I keep telling myself I'll do it the next time we're together, but invariably I get distracted by her smile or her touch or the way we always laugh together, and I decide to put it off.

But she deserves to know the truth and waiting any longer will probably be crossing the line into dishonesty.

Tonight. We have a date already planned, so I'll tell her over dinner, and then hope she still wants to continue the evening with me.

"She's made some calls, trying to locate my father." Rachel's words pull me back into the present conversation. "Not that they'll get any money out of him if they do, but maybe it will speed up the process."

"Then tonight we'll celebrate," I suggest. "Dinner, dessert, romance."

"All of that sounds marvelous." She finishes the last of her chai and picks up the scone to take with her. "Should I meet you here?"

"Nah," I say, shaking my head. "I'll pick you up at Resolution. You're off at six tonight, right?"

She nods, standing and grabbing her purse off the back of the chair. "Am I dressed okay for whatever you've got in mind?"

I pretend to study her for a moment, but truthfully I noticed what she was wearing the moment she walked in… an oversized pink tee shirt that comes halfway to her knees worn over black leggings. Of course, she'd dressed it all up with a long, sparkly necklace and the pretty pink stones in her facial piercings.

"You look great," I say, leaning over to kiss her cheek. "See you at six."

I watch her walk toward the door, not the least bit apologetic for ogling the way her dark wavy hair cascades down her back, landing just above her hips. She stops just before the door and looks back over her shoulder at me. With a wicked grin, I wiggle my eyebrows and wink. She laughs and blows me a kiss.

When she's gone, I take a deep breath and pray that what I have to tell her won't drive her away.

Chapter 26

RACHELLE

I KNOW GABE said I was dressed fine, but that didn't stop me from wanting to put in a little extra effort. So, I ran home on my lunch break to change. The pale pink spaghetti strap dress comes almost to my ankles, but leaves just enough room for my metallic silver sandals to show. Since even summer evenings can be cool in Flagstaff, I put on a lightweight denim jacket to cover my shoulders that are bare thanks to the sleeveless dress. I hope it's sufficient for whatever he has planned in the way of celebrating.

I push open the back door of the tattoo shop and head down the hall to the reception area just as Shane pops out of his room. Naturally, he is the first person to notice the change in my appearance.

"Gabe must've done something right to have you looking like that this afternoon," he says, followed by a wolf-whistle.

"Shut up, you jerk," I reply, but I don't really mean it. I nudge him with my shoulder. "He's picking me up after work, so I changed clothes for our date."

"You've got a date?" Asher asks, sticking his head out of the room.

"Don't act so surprised." I roll my eyes at him. "You have dates all the time."

"With my girlfriend," he says. "Who I'm in a serious relationship with. Are you saying you're in a serious relationship with Gabe?"

"I'm in a relationship with Gabe. This is not news to you."

Asher just laughs and ducks back into his room.

Shane throws an arm around my shoulders and walks toward the front with me. "But is it serious?" he asks, dialing down the goofball vibe and turning up the sincerity. "I like the idea of the two of you."

Shane doesn't often bring out his sweet, endearing side, but I know it's in there.

I sling an arm around his waist and hug him. "It's getting that way."

"Good," he says as we reach the reception desk. "I know it broke your heart that you couldn't have me, so I hope Gabe is a good distraction."

"Get to work, asshole!" It sounds harsh, but I'm laughing as I hurl it at him. He's cackling as he makes his way back down the hall. "You have an appointment at two, remember!"

The rest of the day runs super smoothly, even though Caleb is out for the day. Every client is on time and polite. Several walk-ins show up after lunch and Asher is able to fit them in. Bing hears from Kristy that everything is moving along, and she'll have more details for us soon. Before I know it, my shift is over and Bing is coming out of his office to take over the front desk for the rest of the evening.

"Where are you and Gabe off to tonight?" he asks.

"Not sure." I pick up the denim jacket and slip it on, then grab my purse and fish out my compact. "He said he wants to celebrate the good news that Kristy has found a possible solution to Mom's problems."

Bing nods. "Sounds like Gabe. He's always one to find a reason to have a good time."

"Speaking of good times, tell me about Kristy." I throw it out there casually, like it's not a big deal, but inside I'm dying to know what, if anything, is between them.

"I told you I did some work for her last year." He doesn't look at me when he says it, so I'm certain he's being secretive.

"You know that's not going to fly, *Brett.*" I intentionally use his given name, the same way I heard Kristy refer to him during our meeting. "I could tell by the way the two of you looked at each other that she's more than just a client. I'm asking you how much more."

He sighs, his big shoulders rising and falling. "I'm not sure. I wish I was."

"What's that supposed to mean? Are the two of you seeing each other?"

"It's a complicated situation." He plops down in the chair behind the reception desk and takes a deep breath.

I see the moment he decides to come clean. "Kristy was married before. She's been divorced for about two years. She has a son who's five. She came in February of last year, a few months after her divorce was final. She said the ink was all about her new start. I was pretty taken with her from the first moment, but it took a while to work up the nerve to call and ask her out. When I did, she told me she'd been hoping I would call. We dated for about four months, and it was on the way to being serious. For me it already was."

"You never said anything to me." It's a statement, not a question, because I'm not surprised. Bing holds his cards close to his chest, but I wish he'd felt like he could tell me.

"When there's a kid involved you tread carefully," he answers. "We'd just gotten to the point that she introduced me to him." He smiles, and his eyes look a million miles away. "He's a great kid. Ezra's his name."

"This was last year?" I ask, my voice gentle. "What happened?"

"Her ex reappeared." Bing leans over bracing one elbow on his knee, running his other hand over his buzz cut scalp. "Apologized for cheating and begged for another chance. He said he'd learned his lesson. I was pretty sure he just got dumped by the woman he left Kristy for, but what could I say? She felt like she owed it to Ezra to see if they could put things back together."

"And did they?" I cut my eyes to the front of the building and notice Gabe pulling up to the curb.

Bing shakes his head. "I guess their attempt didn't last long. He hooked up with someone else behind her back. She was too ashamed to call me afterward. When I called her about your mom, she told me the truth. Funny thing is, I don't think she was even surprised that he cheated again."

Gabe is headed to the front door, so I make my next question quick. "So what's your status now?"

Bing shrugs. "We've spent some time together the last couple of weeks. It seems promising, but I'm trying not to let my feelings get ahead of things."

I nod, bending down to give him a quick hug. "I have my fingers crossed for you."

Gabe steps in the door wearing dark jeans and a white button-up shirt. The casually dressy look is incredibly hot on him, and I feel a bit of heat begin to creep up my neck.

"Hey Bing," he says. "You ready, Rach?"

"You bet."

"You guys have fun," Bing calls as we step outside.

I glance over my shoulder and smile at him, hoping maybe he has plans with Kristy later.

DINNER IS ABSOLUTELY fabulous. Somehow, Gabe managed to get reservations at The Brick, an amazing farm-to-table restaurant that just opened a few months ago in historic downtown. It's trendy, but not overly fancy, so thankfully I wasn't underdressed.

We order two completely different entrees so we can share. My grilled chicken breast with orange glaze served with mushroom risotto is delicious, and Gabe's tacos carnitas are both smoky and spicy. I can't remember having a better meal, and though the food is undoubtedly spectacular, I know it's Gabe's company that truly makes it special.

When the check arrives, I almost reach for my purse. There's a part of me that still finds it difficult to let Gabe take care of the total bill. It's not that I'm so progressive or modern that I'm offended by a man taking charge, and I'm certainly not the type of woman who believes she's simply entitled to a man's generosity. It's just that I've taken care of myself for so long that it's strange to let someone else do it. But I've learned over the past few weeks that one of the ways Gabe shows affection is by giving, so it's important that I graciously *receive* from him, because his affections matter.

"I can't believe you were able to get reservations here on such short notice." I reach across the table and touch his hand. He looks up from signing the receipt and smiles. "Thank you, Gabe."

"I made the reservations two weeks ago," he admits, flipping his hand over so he can thread his fingers through mine. "It helps that the manager is a regular at Ugly Mug."

"Two weeks ago?" His thumb is making light circles on my palm, creating enough of a soft buzz in my system that I barely notice the waiter clearing the table.

"Well you know," he begins, "dinner at my apartment and wings with the guys from the shop don't really constitute a proper date with my girl. I was afraid you'd start to think I was a lousy boyfriend."

My girl. It never gets old.

I giggle. I know it's a terribly girly thing to do, but I can't help it. Gabe makes my stomach flutter and my skin heat, and I've never been more aware of my own femininity than when he's showering his attention on me.

It's a heady feeling… one I doubt I'll ever get enough of.

Just then the waiter returns and sits a box on the table. "Your dessert, as ordered. To go."

I cut my eyes to Gabe. I had no idea he'd ordered dessert. He shrugs his shoulders. "I thought we'd take dessert down to Foxglenn Park. We can find a spot with a nice view and enjoy the evening."

"Gabe." I say, taking his hand as he stands and pulls me to my feet. "You're such a romantic."

"You bring it out in me." He leans down and presses a kiss to my forehead.

Walking out of the restaurant, I notice several female glances. Of course I realize they're looking at Gabe. How could they not? But I also figure they're looking at the two of us, at the invisible yet tangible warmth and tenderness that swirls around us. I know this because I've looked longingly at couples before, thinking that kind of connection would never happen for me.

Gabe and his affection came into my life like a whirlwind, a beautiful surprise that I never knew I was hoping for, and as we exit the restaurant I'm certain nothing can spoil the perfect charm of this evening.

I never dreamed I'd be so wrong.

Chapter 27

GABE

THE MAN COMES out of nowhere.

One moment Rachelle and I are turning the corner toward the lot where my car is parked, and the next, the figure of a man steps out from the shadow cast by the building directly into our path.

"Excuse us," I say, slipping my arm around Rachelle and pulling her close.

But he doesn't move.

He lifts his head, and I notice several days' growth of whiskers on his face – not the well-groomed kind. His greasy hair is black, sprinkled heavily with gray, and his skin is dull, like all the color has somehow been siphoned out of it.

But it's his eyes that make me stop. They're sunken and hollow, and yet in a way familiar.

Beside me, Rachelle gasps, a sharp and sudden intake of breath. Her body stiffens against me and all at once I realize who's standing in front of us.

Her father.

"You're a hard bitch to find," he says, his voice slithering and his breath rank with the stale smell of alcohol. "No home address listed anywhere. Had to follow you from that shithole you work at."

I'm momentarily stunned by his appearance out of the blue and the horrible condition he's in, but my mind finally catches up.

"Don't speak to her that way." My voice is soft and calm, yet firm and unyielding. "Now get out of our way."

"Not so fast there, loverboy," he sneers, leaning closer and smacking me in the face with more of his rancid breath. "My daughter and I have some things we need to talk about."

"We have nothing to talk about," Rachelle says, authority ringing in her voice despite the desperate way she's clinging to me.

"You sent the cops out looking for me. I deserve some kind of explanation."

I know he's referring to the investigators Kristy hired, but I suppose to a lowlife criminal, cops and investigators are all the same. Why he's blaming it on Rachelle I have no idea, but I'm sure there's no logical answer where this pathetic excuse for a man is concerned.

"You deserve nothing," she says.

"You're going to talk to me, girl." He takes a step closer and reaches his hand toward her.

It happens so fast that neither one of us has time to react. He grabs Rachelle by the elbow and hurls her forward, yanking her to a stop once she's out of my grasp. She cries out, and I notice his fingers digging into her arm hard enough that I know he'll leave bruises.

I'm not an angry or aggressive person, but in that moment I see red.

I come at him, intending to slam my fist into his face. I can hear the blood rushing in my ears, my pulse pounding as adrenaline floods my system. Before I reach him, he jerks Rachelle forward again. She pushes against him, struggling to free herself from his grip.

"Let go of me!" she screams.

And then, he slaps her. The palm of his hand connects with her cheek with a resounding pop, and Rachelle stumbles backward into the gravel on the other side of the sidewalk. It's like watching in slow motion as she loses her balance, slamming hard into the corner of the building, her shoulder taking the brunt of the impact.

I can't reach her in time, and she lands on her back in the gravel.

The jacket she'd had in her hand is long gone, dropped and forgotten in the struggle. The shoulder strap of her dress is torn, and in the light of the streetlamp, I see blood beginning to pool from a nasty scrape on her shoulder.

"Rachelle!" I shout. The few feet between us seems like miles. Finally making it to her side, I bend down to help her up.

"You sent the cops after me!" her father shouts.

Rachelle now steady on her feet, I turn back to him.

"No, she didn't, but I'm about to if you don't get the hell out of here right now."

Of course, I have every intention of reporting this to the police at the first possible moment, whether he leaves now or not. I just don't inform this dirtbag of it.

"You think you're so much better than me, don't you boy?" He staggers toward me. "You think you can look down your nose at me."

This time I do punch him. Only once, and not as hard as I want to, but I won't deny it feels pretty damn good, especially when he falls and his ass hits the pavement. Hard.

"I *know* I'm better than you," I yell, towering over him as he scrambles backwards on his hands. "You know how I know that? I know it because I watched my dad beat the shit out of my mom for years, and there's not one tiny part of me that would ever consider hurting a woman. Especially Rachelle. So yeah, I'm better than you, asshole!"

I don't know if was the fist to his jaw or the words I shouted at him, but he finally decides to take off, managing to get to his feet and skulking across the street and into the shadows. Were it not for Rachelle behind me, obviously banged up, I'd chase him down and hit him again. It hasn't escaped me that I just laid my worst secret, or at least part of it, out there for her to hear. I want to reassure her that I'm nothing like my father, but the important thing now is to make sure she's okay and call the police.

"Are you all right?" I ask, turning toward her, gently reaching for her hand. "Did you hit your head?"

She shakes her head. "I'm fine." Her voice is shaky, weak, and fragile. I hate it. I hate that my strong, vibrant girl has been reduced to a scared child by that piece of shit. Even worse, I hate that my admission moments before might be part of it. "It's just my shoulder."

I immediately begin untucking and unbuttoning my shirt. She's standing there shivering, holding her dress in place because one strap ripped when she fell. I'll gladly stand here in nothing but an undershirt if it means she's covered and warm.

I'm careful when I put it around her shoulders, helping her slip the uninjured arm into the sleeve. She leaves the other side loose so the fabric doesn't rub against the scrape.

"Blood is going to get on your shirt," she says apologetically.

"Like I give a shit about that." I drape the shirt delicately across the top of her shoulder, avoiding the skin on her shoulder blade. "It's a scrape, so it doesn't need stitches, just some ointment and a bandage. But it'll be wicked sore for a while."

Rachelle just nods, her gaze dropping to the ground.

"We have to call the police," I say.

"I know."

I pull out my cell and make the call and notice the box with our dessert dropped and smashed on the ground. I'm pissed as hell that my plans for the rest of the night were ruined, but now is not the time for my disappointment.

All that matters is keeping Rachelle safe and making sure her father never hurts her again.

Chapter 28

RACHELLE

WE DON'T TALK on the drive back to Gabe's apartment. Neither one of us is sure what to say, and the only sound for miles is the sound of Gabe changing gears. We spent the last hour and a half talking with the police, making sure they had all the information they needed. I suppose we're both talked out.

In my mind I know I should feel anger. I should be all kinds of furious at my father given the many, many ways he's screwed up my life. Mom's life. All the ways he's still screwing us over. But all I feel is numb. My mind isn't even registering the shock of seeing him again after all these years. Maybe it's some kind of self-preservation mode that your body goes into after something awful or traumatic. If it is, I'm grateful for it. And I'm also grateful for Gabe and the way he handled everything when I obviously couldn't.

His hands grip the steering wheel hard enough that his knuckles whiten, and the muscles in his jaw clench and unclench repeatedly. It appears he's mad enough for the both of us. I don't know if his anger is the reason for his silence, or if it has more to do with what he revealed during the confrontation with my dad.

After the shock of seeing my father again, and having him slap me and knock me to the ground, what ever endorphins are responsible for insulating me from total emotional meltdown must also be responsible for learning that Gabe is no stranger to violence. I wonder if he kept it from me out of shame or fear, or maybe a combination of the two.

I understand both.

But could it also be something more?

Going back to Resolution to get my car was never an option. My dad didn't know where I lived, but he knew where I worked and had followed us when we left the shop. No way were we taking chances that he might be waiting there for us.

"I could call Bing to bring my car over," I say, finally breaking the silence. "He could probably get Shane or Caleb to help."

Gabe nods. "I'm sure he would." His voice is clipped, tension lacing each word. "I've got plenty of first aid stuff at my place, so let's get you bandaged up, and then we'll make a plan."

"Okay," I whisper.

Gabe parks behind Ugly Mug, and thankfully all the employees are busy inside so no one sees us arrive. I think if either of us had to answer one more question we might explode. He makes quick work of the two locked doors, and in a matter of seconds we're on our way up the steps to the apartment.

Once we're inside, Gabe walks straight to the bathroom, coming out with a handful of things he takes to the bedroom area. Not sure what to do with myself, I walk over to the living room and drop my purse on the coffee table. I can feel my back muscles beginning to stiffen from the impact of the fall, and the scrape on my shoulder blade is raw and throbbing.

I take a deep breath, telling myself to calm down. I can get through this. He will patch up my shoulder, and then I'll go home and crawl into bed before I fall apart. I can feel tears start to burn behind my eyes, but I hold them back.

I'm still standing by the couch when Gabe comes around the corner of the partial wall concealing his bedroom. His eyes have softened a bit, like maybe some of the fury has worn off, but his body is still wound so tight I wonder if he'll snap.

The snap of a man's temper is something I'm familiar with. Before tonight, I'd only seen it aimed at my mother, and I'm finding it difficult to process that my father turned his anger so easily toward me. I can still feel the sting of his hand on my face, and I bite my lip to keep from groaning.

"Come here, Rach," he says, motioning to where he's standing.

Clutching his shirt closed around me, I make my way to him, unsure of what he's planning. I'm furious with myself for feeling even the slightest bit skittish around

Gabe. Hadn't I told myself over and over again to stop lumping him in with all the bad examples out there? Logically, I know I'm being ridiculous, but when the one man a daughter should be able to trust more than anyone in the world betrays you so heinously, how can that not affect how you relate to other men?

"I laid out a clean shirt for you." He gestures toward the bed and I see another button up shirt, this one a pale yellow, lying on the mattress. "There's a pair of boxer shorts, too."

"Thanks." I step toward the bed, intending to grab them and head to the bathroom to change.

He stops me with a soft touch to my arm. For a split second, a jolt of fear sparks inside me, but as his thumb begins to rub soft circles on the inside of my elbow, I feel myself start to relax. This is *Gabe*, not my father. This is *Gabe*, who has been nothing but kind and generous and sweet to me.

"I'm going to step out to the living room and give Bing a call while you get undressed. But keep the shirt off and lay face down on the bed. I've got some antibiotic ointment and a large bandage."

I take a deep breath and hold it. Shirtless in front of Gabe, even for purposes of bandaging a wound... well, it still conjures up images.

"Yeah, I'll see your naked back, but don't freak out." A hint of a smile plays on his lips, and I'm grateful for the glimpse of *my* Gabe. "I just want to take care of you."

I nod and he exits the bedroom.

I try not to think too much about anything other than getting a bandage on my shoulder as I shed the ruined white shirt, tossing it into an empty laundry basket in the corner. I struggle to get my dress off since I'm hesitant to raise my left arm and flex the shoulder any more than I have to. Eventually, I manage to pull it over my head one-handed, folding the ruined garment and laying it on Gabe's dresser. I twist the strapless bra I'm wearing so that the hooks are in the front, quickly unclipping them and shoving the undergarment between the folds of my dress.

And then I'm standing in Gabe's bedroom in nothing but a pair of pink panties. In my wildest imagination, I would never have dreamed that my father would be the reason I'd be nearly naked in Gabe's apartment for the first time.

Focusing on the task at hand, I slip into the boxer shorts and slide onto the bed, pulling the shirt close so it's within easy reach. I turn my head toward the window so I don't have to meet Gabe's eyes when he rounds the corner.

I can still hear him talking softly. I assume he's on the phone with Bing, so I wait until the talking stops to say anything.

"Ready," I call out, and a second later I hear his footsteps in the room.

"I washed my hands," he says. I hear him at the dresser, unwrapping what I assume is a bandage. "They're clean, I promise."

"I trust you." I whisper, and I realize I mean it. Like… I *really* mean it, from the deepest part of who I am.

He's still for just a moment and then I feel him lean against the bed.

"I'm going to put some antibiotic ointment on it first."

"Okay."

I close my eyes and wait for his touch. I don't realize I'm holding my breath until I feel his fingers on my skin. There's an audible release of the air in my lungs as his gentle touch spreads the ointment over the scrape. I hadn't tried to look over my shoulder at it, but from the feel of Gabe's movements, it must be a pretty big wound.

"The brick wall did a number on your shoulder, Rach," he says. "It's going to feel like crap for a few days."

"I'll live."

"I'm going to put the bandage on now."

It feels almost like a feather as Gabe lays the bandage over the scrape. His fingers are tender as they press around the edges, sealing it to my skin. Once he's finished, I'm suddenly aware that I'm lying shirtless on his bed. I can't decide if it's awkward or intimate.

"At least the shirt won't rub against it too bad now." I hear him rummaging on the dresser. "But don't put it on just yet."

"What?" My voice cracks, completely unsure of his meaning.

"You hit the wall and the ground pretty hard. You're muscles are bound to be sore. If they're not yet, they will be in the morning. I've got some muscle cream that may help."

And then his hands are on my skin, rubbing slow circles on my lower back. Tension I didn't even realize was there begins to ebb, the heat of his hands seeping deep in my muscles. He works his way up my back, stopping just below the bandage on my left side, continuing to my shoulder on the right. The scent of menthol permeates the room. Not exactly the smell I associate with romance, but my muscles begin to unknot and relax.

And so does my mind. At some point, I set aside the notion that I should be wary of Gabe for any reason. So his father was a violent man as well? Does that mean he will be the same? Of course not. If I follow that flawed logic, I'd have to assume I would end up an abuser, too.

Gabe is *not* his father. Of that, I'm certain.

Time sort of stops. I don't doze off, but my mind empties and my body seems suspended in some strange combination of awareness and relaxation. My world narrows to just this moment, with just Gabe and me. His hands on my skin, taking care of me, making sure I'm okay. There's a safety in this moment that I've never known before. My heart is so full it's almost painful, but in an exhilarating kind of way.

Gabe sighs, a heavy deep breath, and then his hands are gone.

"I'll wait for you in the living room," he says, and I hear him step away. When he's almost out of the room, he turns back and whispers, "I know you heard what I said about my father."

I turn my head on the mattress in time to see him disappear around the partial wall of his bedroom. The bathroom door opens and closes, and I hear the water turn on. Sitting up as quickly as I can with my bandaged shoulder, I grab the shirt he left me and slip it over my arms.

Standing from the bed, I glance at myself in the mirror above Gabe's dresser. My hair is a mess and my make-up is long gone. Touching my cheek, I remember the feel of my father's hand slapping me. No redness or any kind of mark is visible, and I'm thankful that at least my face won't bear a physical reminder of his cruelty.

I wait for Gabe to leave the bathroom, before I silently slip inside for my turn. I need a moment to catch my breath and pull myself together before the two of us start unpacking all the unpleasantness this night threw at us. I know I'm going to have to respond to the truth about his father. I'm not angry with him, but it does create another layer for us to navigate through.

I splash my face with water and run a brush through my hair, pulling it into a loose knot with the hair tie around my wrist. Stepping out of the bathroom, I'm still not sure how to begin the conversation, so I step to the window and wait for him to come to me.

Chapter 29

GΛBE

T HE SCRAPE ON Rachelle's left shoulder is nasty, and her dress is ruined. It's better than a cut that would've probably required stitches, but it's going to be really sore for a while.

I could've killed that bastard with my bare hands, and if Rachelle hadn't needed me, I probably would've beaten him to a bloody pulp. Anger still simmers in my gut, but I've got a handle on it. I know Rachelle needs my comfort more than she needs my vengeance.

From the corner of my eye I see her step out of the restroom. Her back is to me as she stares out the window down onto the street below. She's in a pair of my boxer shorts and a button-up of mine, unbuttoned enough at the top to allow the shirt to fall off her left shoulder and not rub against the bandaged wound.

I know she heard what I said during that confrontation with her father. She couldn't have missed the big revelation that I'd watched my own father beat the shit out of my mom. I acknowledged it for half a second before I left her to put the shirt on, and she hasn't said a word since.

God, what she must think of me now.

Silently, I walk over to the window until I'm standing directly behind her. I know she can see my reflection in the glass, but she doesn't turn around, nor does she say anything.

"I'm sorry," I whisper.

She remains quiet, and my soul dies a little. Have I screwed things up beyond repair?

"I know I should've told you." I move closer, enough that my body brushes the back of the oversized shirt she's wearing. When she doesn't scoot away from me, I take it as a good sign. "I should've trusted you. The way you trusted me."

Leaning over, I press my lips against the bare skin of her shoulder, just above the bandage that covers the jagged, angry scrape. She doesn't move, doesn't even flinch.

I press kisses along her shoulder and up her neck until I reach her ear. "I just didn't want you to be afraid of me." My voice shakes, nearly breaking, but I don't care, because there it is. The ugly truth.

I feel her breathe deep, her shoulders moving as she exhales. Slowly, she turns to face me. I close my eyes, afraid of what I might see in her expression. Her hands slide up my chest until her palms rest against both my cheeks. The gentleness in her touch causes a seed of hope to take root in my heart.

"Look at me." Her voice is soft, but steady, and I can

no more deny her than I can stop the earth from turning. "I'm not afraid of you, Gabe. I'll never be afraid of you."

I put my lips to hers and wrap my arms around her, careful not to hurt her already injured shoulder. I don't take it further. I just hold her, our lips pressed together, unmoving. I can't begin to describe the gratitude that fills every cell in my body.

She's still here.

And she's not afraid of me.

"I was so scared you'd think I might turn out like my dad." She shakes her head to argue with me, but I keep going. "And if you thought that, even for a moment, it's okay. I've had those thoughts, too. For so long I was afraid some part of his madness had been passed on to me. Seeing what he did to my mom messed with my self-image in a way I can't even describe. But tonight, when I saw your dad come at you in anger, I knew, beyond any doubt, that I could never be like him. I could never hurt anyone like that. Especially you."

She wraps her arms around me and rests her head against my shoulder. For a long moment, we're silent, just standing together, wrapped up in each other, letting the harsh reality of the night and the honesty of this moment sink in.

"I talked to Bing. He's going to make a plan and get back to us. He mentioned looking at some new security cameras and maybe even getting you a rental car until the police find your dad. I don't think there's any keeping this from the rest of the guys at the shop. They're going to notice all the changes, and you need them on the lookout, anyway," I say, my lips brushing the top of her head. "I doubt he followed us here, but I don't want to take a chance. He followed us from Resolution because he couldn't find your home address, and if there's even the slightest chance he tailed us here, I don't want to lead him to your apartment. Bing and I both think you should just stay here tonight."

I feel her nod against my chest, but she doesn't say anything or look up at me.

"That's not just a line to get you to stay here." I squeeze my arms tighter around her. "I mean, I always want you with me, but if all I wanted was for you to stay the night, I'd just ask."

She pulls back and smiles. "Always the gentleman."

I shrug, happy for a moment of levity. "I try."

"I need to call my mom and let her know."

"I called her while you were in the restroom." I say. "Told her you weren't feeling well and were resting here. She said not to disturb you and just to stay the night."

Her eyes narrow, and I can tell she's not exactly happy that I spoke with her mother.

"I'm sorry if I overstepped. I just wanted to deal with everything for you so you didn't have to talk about if you didn't want to."

"I appreciate that. Really." She steps out of my embrace and walks toward the living room. "But I have to warn her that he's in town. And... I want her to know that what you said was true and not just a cover story for

'I want to bang your daughter tonight'. I don't want her to think I'm being dishonest."

She reaches for her purse on the coffee table and starts digging around, I assume looking for her cell. Afraid that maybe I've offended her, I take her hands and pull her to me before she finds the phone.

"I didn't mean to upset you," I say, tracing circles on the insides of her wrists. "And I get that you want to be up front and honest about the two of us."

"I'm not mad, Gabe," she says. "It's just…"

"But Rach, we're both adults. If we spend the night together, for whatever reason, we don't need anybody's permission."

Chapter 30

RACHELLE

LOOK UP at Gabe and take a deep breath, reaching for my purse again. This is where it gets tricky. How do I make him understand without sounding like a prude or a tease? And why can't I find my stupid phone?

"Rach?" His voice is low, gravelly, and I can tell he's trying to make sense of my actions. I give up trying to find my phone in the abyss that is the inside of my purse and throw it onto the coffee table.

I drop onto the couch, running my hands over my face in frustration. I've never had this conversation before. With other guys, I just cut things off before it got to this point, so I didn't have to go into detail about my choices. I didn't talk about it with other guys because they didn't matter.

But Gabe *matters*. He matters more than I've admitted to myself until this moment.

"When Mom kicked him out," I begin, "him being the piece of trash that was my father, it didn't take her long before she jumped back in the dating pool."

Gabe sits beside me, close enough that his thigh

presses up against mine. He's solid and warm and every greedy molecule in my body reaches out and grabs his body heat.

"I love my mom," I whisper. "So much. She's a high school drop-out with a GED who survived an abusive husband and somehow managed to be a successful single parent. It's more than admirable, and I'm grateful."

Gabe says nothing, just gently places his hand on my knee. Goosebumps spread like wildfire on my skin.

"She was one of *those* women," I say. "She *had* to have a man to feel important or valued. You know the type. They're kind of pathetic, and I generally pity them, but that was Mom for the first few years after Dad split."

"After everything that happened with your father she was probably searching for something positive," Gabe suggests. "She had a bad couple of years. It might not have been smart, but it's understandable."

I nod. "Yeah. I get that now, and to some degree I did even back then. But even at twelve and thirteen years old, I could tell she was making really poor choices. It was like she was so desperate for affection, she'd settle for total douchebags. And, who knows, maybe she thought as long as they didn't punch her in the face or break her ribs they were all right."

"Did any of them hurt her?" His gentle squeeze on my leg sends peace barreling through me. Even though he has to be so completely confused about where I'm heading with this, he's trying to comfort me.

Gabe Jenkins is a god among men. No question.

I shake my head. "Not that I know of. But a few of them stole from her, and trust me, we didn't have a lot for anyone to steal. I'm sure very few of them were faithful to her, but she just kept moving along and tripping into bed with the next man who made her feel special, even if it was all a lie."

I stare toward the front window, gathering my thoughts. Gabe is silent, patient.

"One day I finally forced the issue. Just straight up told her to stop throwing herself at these guys. She deserved so much better and I told her that. I guess no one had ever believed she deserved much of anything and hearing it from me made it sink in." I shift around on the couch so I'm facing him and take a deep breath. "It wasn't long after that when I began noticing boys, and boys started noticing me. I was so careful, Gabe. I've always been so careful to practice what I preached to her. I was careful about who I went out with, who I brought home. And I've never, not even once, treated sex casually."

A pained, uncomfortable expression darkens his face. "I hope you don't think anything about this is casual for me."

"No, no," I race to assure him. "I'm not suggesting that this is something flippant. I know it isn't, for either of us. And I'm certainly not equating you with the jerks my mom dated." Tentatively, I reach up and place my palm against his cheek. "I haven't talked to her a lot about you, about us. I've been selfish with my feelings.

I've wanted to just keep this between you and me, so she has no idea what's between us. If I'm spending the night here because we're playing it safe in case my Dad's wandering around out there, I want her to know that. And if and when I'm spending the night for another reason, well, I want her to know that it's because you're important." I pause, dropping my hand to lace my fingers with his. "If me not being ready to take that step with you yet is a deal breaker, I'll understand."

A softness moves into the edge of his expression, and his eyes drop to our joined hands. "It's not a deal breaker, Rachelle. Not even close."

I tilt my head, searching for his eyes. When his gaze locks with mine, he smiles. Reaching in his pocket, he pulls his own cell phone out and hands it to me.

"Call your mom."

Chapter 31

GABE

SOME PEOPLE MIGHT be surprised that Rachelle Taya, who has facial piercings and works in a tattoo shop, would be so practical and cautious. But I'm not. Relieved and humbled? Yes. Surprised? No. Like me, she grew up early and fast, circumstances making her an adult long before age did.

I was never a player or a man-slut, but I haven't been perfect. Especially the last two years of high school, when I was stuck in Kansas City without my mom. I'd like to think I never led girls on or made promises I had no intention of keeping, but I definitely made the rounds in my social circle. It was how I dealt with my dad's shit after Mom moved away. I just made sure I always had somewhere to go and someone to hang out with. But looking at Rachelle now, knowing she dealt with the same crap I did and seeing how differently she reacted... I wish I'd had her wisdom and foresight. I'm damn grateful she had more sense than me.

Rachelle takes my phone tentatively, her eyes wide as she looks up at me. I can see she's still worried, thinking that I'm going to bolt just because she told me she wasn't ready to sleep with me yet.

Hoping to get rid of that anxiety, I lean down and press my lips to hers. The kiss is soft and comforting. When I pull away, I leave my forehead pressed against hers, my eyes level with her gaze.

"There's not much that could break this deal we've got going, babe," I whisper. "Unless you're a closet serial killer or some kind of terrorist, I'm all in."

"Gabe," she breathes, and I kiss her again, just because I want to.

"If you want a little privacy, use the bedroom." I stand, pulling her to her feet along with me. "After you talk to your mom, I'll tell you whatever you want to know about my family."

But even as the words leave my mouth, I know there's part of it I'll leave out. I'm not sure if it's me or her I'm hoping to spare from the ugliness, but the fact of the matter is, I'm a chicken shit.

Rachelle makes quick work of calling her mom, and then she's back on the couch with me, snuggled into my side.

"Just tell me whatever you want to," she says. "I know from experience it's hard to answer questions sometimes, so just tell me the story however you need to tell it."

I feel like she just gave me permission to omit the parts I don't want to tell her. Even though I know I'm imagining that I'm somehow off the hook for parts of the truth, I go with it anyway.

"The first time I remember seeing my dad hit my mom was when I was in the third grade. I know it had to have been going on before then, but I guess he was more discreet, and my mom was good at shielding me from it."

I shift around, pulling her closer and threading my fingers into her hair. She's quiet. She doesn't ask questions. She doesn't push. She just waits.

"We were on vacation in San Francisco. I remember being at a restaurant and, for whatever reason, my father kept getting more and more agitated. He was in a big hurry to get out of there. I had to go to the restroom, so Mom walked with me and waited outside the door. I tried to be quick because I could see how upset he was, but I wasn't quick enough. When we got back to our hotel room he and Mom argued, and it escalated quickly. When he hit her I remember being scared, but not really surprised. I remember realizing then what a difference there was between an open palm and a closed fist."

In response, Rachelle simply lays her head against my shoulder; her presence is both a comfort and a miracle.

"That sort of thing continued over the years. Mom kept as much of it away from me as she could, but I always knew when he'd hit her. She'd suddenly wear long sleeves five days in a row, or her make-up would be darker than usual, stuff like that. At some point he started adding alcohol to the mix. Not that he'd ever been a tee-totaler or anything, but somewhere along the way he started drinking really heavily at home, and let's just say violent *and* drunk is a nasty combination."

Beside me, I hear Rachelle's quick intake of breath. Remembering the stench of alcohol on her father's breath, I know she's acquainted with the effects of alcohol on an already abusive man.

"When I was fifteen he went too far. He beat her up so badly that she needed medical attention. The fight ended with him shoving her through a sliding glass door. Going to the hospital was out of the question because regardless of how many lies he told, someone would figure out what had really happened. So my grandmother made a few phone calls and got some doctor she knew to come over and treat my mom. I don't know what sort of blackmail material she had on the guy, but he agreed to not breathe a word of what he'd seen. Mom had several broken ribs, a concussion, and a broken wrist, along with quite a few cuts that required stitches."

"Gabe," she whispers, leaning up to press a soft kiss to my jaw. She doesn't say she's sorry or that she under-stands, even though I know she does. She just lets me know she's here.

"I knew she had to leave him. If she didn't he was going to wind up killing her. But when I tried to talk to her about it, she wouldn't even discuss it. His family's loaded, and he could hire a team full of lawyers. She knew he'd never let her leave and take me with her, and she wasn't about to leave me behind. My grandmother, who I now refer to only as Sylvia, offered Mom a shit ton of money to leave. Sylvia isn't evil like my father. It's just that all that matters to her is appearances. Everything has to *appear* perfect, even if it's rotten on the inside. She knew that she wasn't going to be able to contain the situation much longer, and the perfect Jenkins image was going to crash and burn once the truth became public knowledge. The offer of money was just damage control for Sylvia, and it made Mom angrier and even more determined not to leave."

"But she did leave, right?" It's the first question she's asked, but still it's not pushy or invasive.

"I sat her down and finally made her see reason. My father had never laid a hand on me. He wasn't nice or loving, but he'd never been violent toward me. Besides that, I was fifteen and just about as big as he was. I kept myself busy with my friends and after school things, so I wasn't home a lot. I had two and a half years left before I turned eighteen, at which time I was leaving Kansas City anyway, so why shouldn't she get a head start? She said she couldn't take the money. I asked her why the hell not. I told her she'd earned every cent and then some and giving her enough money to start a new life was the absolute least my father's family owed her."

"It couldn't have been easy to leave you behind."

"Hardest day of my life was watching her leave that day. But it kept her safe and got her out of a situation that would've eventually killed her. The divorce was quick and uncontested. She chose Flagstaff because she has a cousin here. As soon as she got settled and I knew she was going to stay, I started looking at possible colleges in the area."

"You never thought of going somewhere else?" she asks.

I shake my head. "I think I knew on some level that college wasn't going to be my path. It just took me a while to be okay with that because college is what's expected of you when you have good grades and have potential. I think I just needed somewhere to land for a while, long enough to figure out what direction I was headed. What better place to do that than here with my mom?"

"Your mom's doing great, isn't she?"

"Yeah. It took a year or so before she felt really safe, but eventually her life here became her normal, and the ugliness became a memory."

Rachelle snuggles closer and takes a deep breath. She doesn't say anything. Instead, she lets the silence settle around us. After a night full of tension and unpleasantness, this moment is a breath of fresh air.

"I like this normal," Rachelle whispers, wrapping her arm around my waist.

"Me too," I whisper.

And then we fall asleep, wrapped up together on my couch.

Chapter 32

GABE

SOMETIME AFTER MIDNIGHT I woke up and reluctantly settled Rachelle in my bed and myself on the sofa with a pillow and blanket. Thankfully, I slept soundly knowing she was just a few feet away, safe from her father and all his malice.

I wake up at seven, despite the fact that I'm not on the schedule at Ugly Mug this morning. A quick peek at Rachelle assures me she's still resting, so I quietly walk to the kitchen to see what I have in the way of breakfast.

The single box of cereal and three granola bars that are probably six months old make it obvious that I manage a coffee shop and rarely eat breakfast at home. I glance over at my coffee pot and wonder when I used it last. A bag of coffee beans sits on the counter beside the pot, but no way do I want to put those in the grinder and wake Rachelle up with all that noise.

Accepting the fact that I'm not equipped to cook breakfast, I pull out my cell and text Grace.

Me: *Can you discreetly bring me two large coffees with hazelnut and two of whatever scones are fresh?*

*And don't let Harrison or any of the others see you
coming up here. Please?*

Grace: *Be right up.*

I thank my lucky stars that Grace was on the schedule to open today. No way would I have asked anyone
else to bail me out on breakfast. She's about to finish
cosmetology school, so I know her days at Ugly Mug are
numbered. Pretty soon she'll be starting her career. I'm
super proud of her, but dang, I'm going to miss her.

I stand by the door, listening for footsteps on the
stairs. When I hear her approaching, I pull the door open
slowly and step out onto the landing.

"Rachelle?" Grace asks, her tone soft and unassum-
ing. She slips the bag with the scones over my wrist,
leaving my hands free for the coffees.

I nod. "But it's not what you think. She had a shitty
night, so she crashed here."

"Is she okay?"

"Yeah. Family drama. Really unpleasant. Thanks for
bringing this stuff," I say, gesturing to the coffee and
scones. "I have shit for breakfast up here because I always
wind up eating downstairs. I didn't want anyone getting
the wrong idea."

"No problem." She turns to head back down to the
shop. "Let me know if you need anything else."

Slipping back inside my apartment, I set our breakfast on the coffee table just as Rachelle peeks around the
corner.

"Is that coffee I smell?" she asks, her voice still full of

sleep.

"Did I wake you?"

She shakes her head. "No. The shoulder did. But if there's coffee and scones, I'm glad I'm awake."

"There's ibuprofen in the bathroom cabinet," I say, stepping toward her with every intention of kissing her good morning.

She stops me a foot away from her with a hand on my chest. Her other hand covers her mouth. "Don't come any closer. Morning breath. I hope you won't mind if I borrow your toothbrush."

I chuckle. "You're welcome to my toothbrush and anything else in there, but hang on a second." Moving to the kitchen, I riffle through my junk drawer until I come across the freebie toothbrush I got a couple of weeks ago at the dentist's office. "You can have this one. Just leave it in there."

She narrows her eyes, and I realize that I've just done the equivalent of telling her to leave a toothbrush here. Not wanting her to think I'm assuming or expecting too much, I scramble to clarify. "Not that I think you'll be needing a toothbrush here on a regular basis. I just happened to have a new one and figured you might as well use it."

She smiles, and then laughs, so I figure she's not freaked out. "Nothing wrong with having a toothbrush here, just in case."

I watch as she disappears into the bathroom, struck once again with how stupendously fortunate I am that she's with me. Closing my eyes, I remember our dessert, smashed and destroyed on the sidewalk last night, and my plans for the rest of the evening derailed by the appearance of her father.

An idea forms in the back of my mind, and I decide to go with it. It might not be as perfect or romantic as what I'd hoped to create last night, but why should her deadbeat dad get to completely ruin our weekend?

The blanket and candles I'd packed for our dessert picnic are still in the back of my Jeep, so I grab the blanket I used last night from the couch and quickly spread it on the floor by the coffee table. I rummage through the cabinet until I manage to find a couple of small jar candles. By the time Rachelle emerges from the bathroom I've dimmed the lights, lit the candles, and started Sinatra playing softly.

"Gabe?" she asks. "What's all this?"

"We missed dessert last night." I shrug my shoulders and grin at her. "I thought I'd make it up to you with breakfast."

Chapter 33

RACHELLE

GABE THROWS A couple of pillows from the sofa onto the blanket and helps me have a seat on the floor. Not that my injured shoulder would make it difficult to sit down, but he's being so gentlemanly that I don't stop him.

"It's not the strawberry napoleon that we would've had last night," Gabe says, pulling the scones from the bag and placing them on a plate.

"I never complain about orange cranberry scones," I reply. "They're my favorite."

He smiles, and my heart does its normal flip-flop. "I know. I'm glad that's what was on the menu this morning."

Several minutes later, the scones and coffee are gone, and I start to gather the trash. Gabe stops me when I try to get up to throw things away.

"Wait," he says, grabbing everything and putting it back on the coffee table.

I'm still in Gabe's yellow-button up and boxer shorts. Of course, they're both too big for me, but I'm enjoying the feeling of being wrapped up in him. Though the bandage protects the scrape on my back, one side of the shirt still hangs slightly off my shoulder.

I sit up straight as Gabe scoots closer. He reaches to touch the bare skin exposed by the shirt. "You mind if I check the bandage?"

I shake my head and start to turn around, my heart rate kicking up a notch at the feel of his soft fingers against my skin.

"You don't have to turn around," he whispers. "Just lean your head on my shoulder."

Gabe holds me gently, and the position is incredibly intimate. My cheek rests against his shoulder as he reaches around to move the shirt. His fingers trace the outline of the bandage, causing goosebumps to break out across my skin. I feel each of his breaths against my flesh, my own breath becoming shallow and quick.

"It didn't bleed through the bandage," he says, leaning back enough to look at me, but keeping our faces close.

It takes my brain a moment to catch up, but eventually I manage to speak. "That's good. I'm glad I didn't ruin another one of your shirts."

"You know I wasn't worried about my shirts." He presses a kiss to my forehead.

"Thank you." My voice is a whisper, the words soft and tender between us. "For taking such good care of me."

He smiles, and it's unlike any smile I've seen before.

The depth of joy in his expression takes my breath away.

"I wanted to tell you something last night." He reaches out to push a strand of hair behind my ear. "I had this whole plan. Dessert at the park under the stars. I had a blanket and candles in the back of my Jeep."

"Then my Dad ruined everything."

Gabe's laugh is soft, his eyes still filled with emotions so intense I can't name them.

Then his words register.

I wanted to tell you something last night.

All sorts of possibilities race through my brain, but I shove them back, refusing to allow my speculation to run away from me. Maybe he just wanted to tell me plans for our next date. Or maybe he wanted to talk about the new tattoo he's been designing with Asher. Maybe he decided...

"I'm in love with you, Rachelle."

My train of thought comes to a screeching halt just as my heart accelerates like a bullet. The tiny bulb of hope that sprouted a moment ago takes off, opening wide until my heart is in full-bloom.

Both Gabe's hands come up to gently frame my face, his thumbs tracing the skin beneath my eyes. "I love you," he repeats, his forehead coming to rest against mine.

His words... the sweetness of his sentiment... the genuine emotion shining in his eyes... I take it all, gathering it close, and wrapping it up and pulling it deep into my heart, memorizing every sight, every feeling, every sound. I never, ever want to lose the beauty of this moment.

"Rach?" he whispers. "I hope the fact that you're speechless is a good thing."

I should respond. I know I should. I don't want to leave him out there all alone on that very scary ledge. It takes a moment for the signal to travel from my brain to my vocal cords, but I finally make it happen.

"I love you, Gabe," I manage to say. And then I kiss him.

I don't know how it's possible to kiss and smile at the same time, but Gabe does it. I know this because I can feel his smile against my lips. Laughter, the kind that's sweet and secret, bubbles between us, and we're both grinning like idiots when we pull apart.

"I didn't expect you, Gabe." I thread my fingers through the blond hair at the back of his neck. "You've been such a surprise in my life. Such a wonderful surprise."

"I want to keep on surprising you." He pulls both my hands to his lips and kisses each palm. "I want to keep on making you happy."

"Okay." The word slips out as I swallow past the huge lump in my throat. I think, in his own way, Gabe is offering me forever, even though neither one of us is ready to start throwing that word around yet. I take a deep breath and go on. "It goes both ways, you know. I want to make you happy, too."

"So we just go right on making each other happy," he says. "Deal?"

"Deal," I agree.

And the kissing and stupid grinning recommences.

Chapter 34

RACHELLE

THE GUYS ARE smothering me. Seriously. It's like I can't go pee without one of them following to make sure I'm okay. I will admit that it's sweet. I have no idea what it's like to have brothers, but I'm guessing it's something like this.

"Your new ride's out back, Rach," Shane calls from the hall. "And it's sweet!"

Bing insisted that I drive a different car until this is settled. My dad knows very few details about my life, but he does know where I work and what I drive. Thus, the alternate vehicle.

"Holy crap!" I nearly shout. My mouth drops open at the sight of Bing standing next to a black Mini Cooper sitting in my normal spot behind Resolution. It seems being a tattoo artist has its perks because Bing knows people in all lines of work, and they are all willing to do him a favor.

"It's just back off lease," Bing says. "Jared says you can drive it as long as you need."

I assume Jared is the car dealer who's cool enough to

loan me a car. I'm sure my Focus looks just dandy sitting on his lot of super hot cars like this Mini.

"This better not be costing you a fortune, Bing. I could've driven a rusty beater for a lot less money."

Bing just shakes his head. "No worries. Next time he comes in the shop, his ink's on me, so I'm not out anything."

The barter system is alive and well in the tattoo industry it seems.

Caleb's truck wheels into the parking lot, he and Asher returning from lunch.

"Look at Rach's car!" Shane hollers as they jump out of the truck.

"It's not my car!" I say, elbowing Shane in the ribs. Looking out toward Asher and Caleb, I say, "It's only temporary."

"Might as well enjoy it," Caleb says, with a wink. "Besides, you'll look super hot driving that thing around."

"Don't let Gabe hear you say that." Asher smacks Caleb on the back of the head. "He might poison your coffee."

"Grace would look hot driving it, too," Caleb laughs and jumps back when Asher swings at him half-heartedly.

Grace is Asher's girlfriend. They've been together for over a year, but they've been in love with each other longer than that. Asher is well and truly smitten, and I won't be surprised if he puts a ring on Grace's finger sooner rather than later.

"There are two new motion sensor lights out here." Bing points toward the light pole at the corner of the lot and then to the fixture above the door. "So the parking lot should never be dark. There's also a camera mounted on the other side of the door that points directly at your car. It feeds to my phone and my laptop and alerts me if there's movement. But even with all that, I still don't want you walking out here alone. One of us will always come with you and check things out."

"Four tatted up guys to watch out for you." Shane says, throwing an arm around me.

"Five when Dex is around," Caleb adds, reminding Shane to include our body-piercing guy.

"I hate all this fuss," I say. "But you guys really are awesome."

"We love you, Rach," Shane replies.

"Yeah, we do." Gabe's voice comes from behind me. He pushes Shane out of the way and pulls me into his embrace. "Hands off my girl, Shane."

"Yes sir," Shane laughs, raising one hand in a mock salute.

"We were just discussing the precautions we're taking around here," Bing says, going on to point out the new lights, the camera, and the loaner car.

Gabe nods in approval. "And when she's not at work, I'm on security detail."

When I think back on my childhood, about watching my father's violence and my mother's string of loser boyfriends, it's hard to believe that I'm standing here surrounded by five strong, loyal, and incredibly decent men. And though being the center of such attention is never my favorite thing, having all these guys care for me and want to help me is something I'll never get over or take for granted.

Bing's phone dings with a text. "Kristy's on her way."

Asher, Shane, and Caleb have all been brought up to speed on the situation. The only thing they aren't aware of is the fact that Bing and I are half siblings, but I've decided it's time they knew that truth as well, so as soon as we're finished meeting with Kristy, I'm coming clean with them.

Caleb's next appointment isn't for another hour, so he takes a seat at the front desk just in time to welcome Asher and Shane's next appointments. As he's getting everything in order for them, Kristy pops in the front door, and she, Gabe, Bing, and I close ourselves in Bing's office.

"Settling the debts through bankruptcy will be relatively painless," Kristy says. "Like most things in the legal system, it may seem to move at a snail's pace, but credit card debt is much easier to deal with than real estate or other tangible assets. Once that's done, we can move pretty quickly with divorce proceedings."

It doesn't surprise me the way Bing's eyes linger on Kristy, and I'm more than a little pleased to see the small smile that crosses her face when she catches his gaze. Kristy is a classic beauty, golden blonde hair drawn back into a sleek ponytail at the nape of her neck. Her choco-late brown skirt hits the tops of her knees, and the bright coral blouse with small ruffles around the collar is sexy without being revealing.

They couldn't look more opposite, especially with Bing's buzz cut hair and full sleeve tattoos, but some-thing about the two of them just clicks.

"So, now we wait. The paperwork is in motion, and the investigators have been informed to step up their surveillance in the area. I doubt that with his limited resources your father has been able to travel very far."

"I can't tell you how much my mother and I appreci-ate all your help." It's a pitiful offering of gratitude for all she's done and continues to do, but it's all I've got.

Kristy nods. "At some point I'll need to sit down with your mother in person again. I'll give Brett a call next week, and we can set something up."

Brett. I know it's his given name, but the way she uses it sounds like a term of endearment.

Beside me, Gabe places a hand on my knee and squeezes. I know he's also noticed the warmth between Bing and Kristy.

When Kristy stands, the rest of us do as well, shaking hands and saying *thanks* all over again.

"I've got to pick up Ezra, but I'll be in touch." It comes across as a general statement, but I know it's directed toward Bing. She means she'll call *him* later.

I'm so incredibly happy that my brother may be on his way to happiness.

Chapter 35

GABE

UGLY MUG IS going up for sale.

Marshall and Janie told me this morning. They're retiring and selling both shops. They assured me that they want to find a buyer that intends to keep things running in much the same way, but there's no guarantee. A new owner might not want to keep the current staff – including me – employed.

A sick feeling works its way into the pit of my stomach. Not exactly how I wanted to start my morning. Mom's on her way to the shop for coffee and catch-up time, and I'm going to be in a foul mood and unable to hide it.

Determined to at least have things ready for her, I head over to the waffle iron. I'm not the cook, but I can manage waffles and fruit for Mom.

By the time Mom arrives, I've set a table in the back of the room, closest to the steps leading upstairs, with her breakfast, a vanilla latte, and my straight black coffee. I'm hoping it'll burn away the dread in my gut.

After the usual hugs of greeting, Mom dives right in.

"Spill it, son. I can tell something's bugging you. It's not Rachelle, is it?"

"No, not Rachelle." A sliver of the self-pity I'd been gnawing on slides away when I remember that whatever else may happen, I have the woman I love. "Marshall and Janie are going to sell Ugly Mug."

Mom doesn't bat an eye. "That doesn't surprise me. They've worked all their lives and built two thriving businesses. Now with their kids grown they want more freedom and less responsibility."

"It could cost me my job." I gulp down half my coffee at that sour thought.

"It could," Mom says. "Or you could buy the place."

She says it so matter-of-factly that it takes me a moment to process it.

"I can't afford it on my salary." The words are a lousy ploy to divert her attention away from where her thoughts were.

"You can afford it," she counters, pointing a fork full of strawberries across the table at me. "You have money."

"Mom, you know I've never wanted a cent of that money." I down the rest of my coffee. "The only good thing I've ever wanted to do with it is help Rachelle and her mom."

"Stupid boy." Mom shakes her head. "Don't you think it'll help Rachelle if you have a stable career owning a successful business? And there's no question you have the skills to do it."

"It's like acknowledging that he exists." My voice

drops to a whisper. I don't have to tell her I'm talking about my father. She knows.

But my mother is relentless. "You earned that money just as much as I earned what Sylvia paid me when I left. Besides, your grandfather was a decent man. Not a saint by any means, but not superficial and fake like Sylvia and certainly not a monster like your father. He set up that trust fund when you were a baby because he wanted you to always be taken care of. Part of me has always wondered if he somehow suspected that his no good son might ruin it all."

"Mom, I just don't know if I can."

"I don't know why the hell not," she says, echoing the words I said to her when Sylvia offered her a financial payout to divorce my father and leave.

I can't help the chuckle that escapes me. It's hard to argue with my mom and my fifteen year-old self who'd convinced her that she had to go before dad killed her.

I'd been right about that.

Maybe she's right about this.

Could I own this business? Sure I could. I run it by myself now without really breaking a sweat most days. I could add on the responsibilities of owner and delegate a few of the managerial duties to Harrison.

And just like that I've gone from twenty-something employee to someone with a potential career-path.

But still, it's a lot to think about, so I slow the crazy thought train down a bit. "I'll consider it, Mom."

Satisfied that she's made her point, she reaches across

the table and pats my hand, then returns to her waffle.

The rest of our visit centers on her job at the pottery studio and my relationship with Rachelle. I stop short of telling her that Rach and I now use the "L" word – that's just between us – but I do tell her that things have moved from beginner to serious status, and that Rachelle isn't going anywhere any time soon. Or ever if I have my way.

"Then you have to tell her the rest of the truth," Mom says in response.

I sigh. "I know. I keep waiting for the right moment."

"There's never a right moment to tell someone that your father is a murderer, but keeping it from her isn't right, Gabe. Especially if the two of you are as serious about each other as you say."

She's right. Again.

"Okay," I agree. "I'll tell her soon."

Chapter 36

RACHELLE

"**G**UYS, CAN YOU hang around for a few?" I call down the hall as I flip the sign on the front door to *closed*.

It's rare that everyone, minus Dex since he's only here a few days a month, is here at the end of the day. Most of the time the guys' appointments finish up at different times, and unless one of them hangs around to pick up the random walk-in, they head out as soon as they're done.

I decide the fact that tonight they each ended right at closing time is a sign. I've kept the truth about Bing and me from them long enough.

"Sure thing," Shane shouts back.

"Everything okay?" Asher asks, stepping out of his room and closing the door.

"Everything's fine," I answer. "Just want to let you guys in on something important."

From the corner of my eye I catch Bing looking at me from his office. He's wanted to tell them the truth for some time. I was the one that kept holding out. His slight nod tells me he knows what I'm planning and that he approves.

"Are you engaged?" Shane says with excitement, exiting his room to stand with Asher in the hallway.

"I've got a hundred bucks that says she is," Caleb puts in, also coming out of his room to stand with his buddies.

"You'd lose," I say matter-of-factly, turning the deadbolt and killing the light in the lobby. "Head to the break room and I'll fill you in."

Bing follows me down the hall, and once we're all in the small break room, I dive right in.

"Caleb, you were here when I started at Resolution," I begin. "And Shane, you came on a few months after I started."

They both nod in agreement and look curious as to where I'm going.

"The shop's reputation was spreading and things were really beginning to pick up. I felt like the weak link most of the time."

"That's stupid, Rach," Caleb interrupts. "You were a pro from the jump, keeping the schedule *and* us organized and in line."

"Thanks, Caleb." I'm aware that my insecurities were exaggerated in my mind during that time, but his affirmation is nice to hear.

"I can't imagine you as a weak link," Asher adds. "Ever."

"I realize now that most of it was just in my head,

but there was a learning curve and it took me a while to adjust."

"Why don't we sit down?" Bing suggests, grabbing one of the chairs from the table and flipping it around backwards. "You're all probably going to have questions, so we might as well be comfortable."

"So you know what this is all about?" Shane takes a chair and does the same thing. Caleb and Asher follow suit, which makes me the only one sitting the *normal* way in my chair.

"Yeah, I do." Bing turns to me. "Why don't I tell the rest of it, since it started with me."

"Okay," I say, nodding my head. "But before you do, I want the guys all to know that it was my idea to hold back. Not because I don't trust all of you, but because of my own hang-ups."

"My mom got pregnant with me when she was in high school," Bing starts. "You're all probably aware of that. I never knew my biological father. As I got older, I started asking questions. Eventually, she told me about my father, and it wasn't good. Turns out it was a good thing he was absent from my life. But that didn't stop me from wondering. So, I started digging around, looking for information about him. I found out that eventually he got married, though the marriage wasn't happy and fell apart thanks to his asshole tendencies."

Bing pauses to take a breath.

"I get the sense this is all leading up to something." Asher phrases the statement like a question.

"It is." Bing props his elbows on the back of the chair and leans forward. "In all that digging around, I found out I had a sister. She was fourteen at the time, and even though I was a grown man, it took me most of a year to work up the nerve to go meet her. Unlike me, she'd had the misfortune of growing up, at least for eleven years of her childhood, with our father, and I didn't know if she'd want anything to do with me."

"Seriously?" Shane practically yells.

"Are you kidding me?" Caleb smacks the table.

"No way!" Asher says.

Their simultaneous outbursts tell me they've figured it out.

"You two are brother and sister?" Caleb asks once the shock has worn off.

"Yes," I answer. "And it was me who kept it from you, not Bing. At first it was because I wanted so badly to fit in, to do a good job and be accepted on my own merit. After a while, it just became easier not to talk about it because then we didn't have to think about our no-good father."

"But now he's back," Bing says. "And causing problems for Rach and her mom, which causes problems for me."

Shane runs a hand through his tousled blond hair, which has been surprisingly free from its normal gelled spikes the past few days. "It's going to take a little time to get used to the fact that the two of you are half-siblings," he says. "But you have to know it doesn't change the way we feel about either of you. You pull your weight around here as much as the rest of us, Rach. Probably more so. No one would ever say you're here just because you're Bing's sister."

"You guys are my family." I make a point to look each of them in the eye. "As much as Bing and my mom. I love each of you." Landing on Asher, I add, "Grace, too. And I hate that this business with my parents is affecting all of you."

"We've got your back," Asher says.

"He's a loose canon," Bing says, referring to our father. "That makes him dangerous. But he's not smart and he doesn't have money, so hopefully that means the amount of damage he can do is limited."

"He's done enough damage already. The reason he showed back up after all this time is because Kristy, the attorney who was here earlier today, has investigators looking for him. It's a really complicated story, but the short version is that he and my mom are still legally married, and he's run up several credit card bills that she's now being held responsible for, because he isn't paying them and the companies can't find him."

Shane mutters a curse. Asher shakes his head in disbelief.

"Can we help at all?" Caleb asks.

"Just keep an eye on Rachelle until everything settles," Bing says. "Between the four of us and Gabe, she'll be safe. If we can just neutralize the asshole, Kristy can deal with the financial end of things and get the divorce taken care of."

Chapter 37

GABE

TWO WEEKS LATER and there's been no sign of Rachelle's father. The two of us have carved out time together when we can, but she's understandably been keeping close to her mom.

Today, I cut out of Ugly Mug around three o'clock to take coffee and snacks over to Resolution. Rachelle's mom is there meeting with Kristy, so I fill one of the large take out containers with coffee and grab one of the boxes with cups, sugar, and cream.

As I'm about to head out, Grace hands me a bag of cookies. "Chocolate chip and pecan shortbread," she says. "Say hi to Asher for me."

"Will do," I nod. "Thanks."

Ten minutes later, I'm parked at the curb in front of Resolution, unloading the supplies from my Jeep, when I hear the front door open.

"Need some help?" Rachelle asks.

She looks like a dream in a yellow oversized tank top. Her smooth skin and bright smile make my heart bounce wildly in my chest. You'd think by now I'd be used to how beautiful she is, but every time I look at her it knocks me in the gut all over again.

"From you, always."

She greets me with a hug and a soft kiss to the lips. Mindful that we're on the sidewalk in full view of everyone on the street, I keep it PG and cup her cheek with the hand that's not holding the coffee.

"Wow," she says, pulling back to look in the backseat. "Did you bring the whole shop?"

"Just coffee and cookies." I grab the coffee supplies and she takes the bag of cookies. "It's easier to do coffee in one of these to-go boxes than to try and haul eight individual cups over here."

"Well, the guys will be stoked for Ugly Mug delivery." She takes the bag with the cookies and heads back toward the door. "We can set it up at my desk."

"How's the meeting going?" I ask as the two of us arrange everything behind the counter, setting cups, coffee accessories and the cookies next to the big container of coffee.

"Not sure. She needs to handle as much of this as she can herself, so I'm staying out of this one."

"What about Bing and the guys?" I take her hand and pull her closer to me.

She laces her fingers with mine. "All with clients. It's been a full schedule today."

"So," I begin with a grin, cutting my eyes toward the front door to make sure no one's headed in. "We're all alone."

Her smile is brilliant as I lower my lips to hers and wrap my arms around her. This is one of those moments we've managed to find amid the chaos, and I'm grateful for it.

Until a loud throat clearing lets us know we're not by ourselves anymore.

"Sorry guys," Asher snickers. "Can you get Ozzy taken care of, Rach?"

Rachelle moves to the computer to print out the aftercare instructions for the tall, burly man with black plastic wrapped around what I'm sure is a sick piece of ink on his left forearm.

"Coffee man?" I nod to indicate the stuff Rach and I set up.

"Absolutely." Asher grabs a cup.

"Grace says hi."

The smile that crosses his face is something I might've once ribbed him about, but not anymore. Not now that I know the feeling behind it.

"Can I tell you a secret?" Asher asks.

"Of course." We step away from the counter where Rachelle is taking Ozzy's payment and walking him through the next few days of itching and flaking.

"I mean, like top secret," Asher continues. "Like you can't say anything to anyone. Not even Rachelle."

"My lips are sealed, bro."

Asher reaches in his jeans pocket and pulls out a small velvet box, and suddenly I get why this is so top secret. With our backs to the counter, he flips it open to reveal the sparkling diamond engagement ring inside. I know next to nothing about jewelry and quality and all that, but it's pretty, and I know Grace will love it.

"Ash," I say, nudging him with my shoulder. "Congrats."

He grins like an idiot and sticks the ring back in his pocket.

"When are you going to do it?"

"Tonight," he whispers. "I'm done here in a couple of hours. I'm picking her up and heading to Lowell Observatory. Looking at the stars is kind of our thing. I'm gonna ask her there."

Some will say they're too young – Asher's twenty-one and Grace is nineteen – but those two have loved each other for a long time, and not one of us who knows them doubts for a moment that they're meant to be together. Besides, Ash has an established career and Grace is about to finish cosmetology school. Those two are on their way, professionally and personally.

"Did you ask her parents for their blessing?" I ask, mostly out of curiosity. Some people find that an outdated tradition, but I figure sometimes it's the right thing to do.

"Sort of. I told them that I love Grace with all my heart and the two of us were committed to each other for the long haul. I said I hoped they'd approve and give their blessing when the time came for me to ask her to marry me. They said they would."

"Asher," Rachelle calls over to us. "Your next appointment just pulled up."

Sure enough, a guy about our age is climbing out of his car, which is parked directly behind mine. He's a total hipster with his beard and shaggy hair, and I'd bet money this is his first tattoo.

"I bet he wants a peace sign," Asher says, chuckling under his breath.

"Good luck tonight. I know she'll say yes." I keep my voice low so Rachelle doesn't overhear as she's getting hipster dude signed in and ready to go.

As Asher heads back to his room, Bing and his latest appointment walk in to the lobby. The brunette is probably in college, based on the NAU tee shirt she's wearing, and she's looking at Bing adoringly. Rachelle intercepts her before she can hang all over Bing. Rach is good like that, keeping the ladies who might fawn all over their tattooist occupied so the flirting and innuendo don't get out of hand.

Good thing, too, since Kristy and Rachelle's mom choose that moment to emerge from Bing's office and into the lobby with the rest of us.

Bing steps over to Kristy, but not too close. "You guys get things taken care of?"

Jennifer smiles and shakes Kristy's hand. "Ms. Fletcher is a smart lady, and I feel so much better with her in charge."

As Bing and Kristy begin a soft conversation not meant for the rest of us, Jennifer walks over and hugs Rachelle. Then she hugs me. I figure I've passed the mom test.

"I know that none of what she's doing is simple," Jennifer says, "but I wish I'd known that I had options. Maybe then I wouldn't have waited so long to get some help. She's a lifesaver."

"This is why you can't keep things from me, Mom. Hopefully nothing like this happens again, but if you find yourself in a situation you're not sure how to handle, tell me. I may not have all the answers, but between Bing, Gabe, and me, we know a lot of people. We can find out."

I'm secretly thrilled that she included me in that statement.

"Believe me, I've learned my lesson this time," Jennifer says. "Now, I know you two haven't spent a lot of time together lately, so I want you to do something tonight. Bing is going to drive me home and make sure everything is okay at the duplex. Mr. Grainger will be right next door if I need anything."

From the corner of my eye I notice Bing walking Kristy out. Something's definitely brewing hotter there. And Jennifer pushing Rach and me together for the night while at the same time making reference to Mr. Grainger, the landlord? Yeah, I'm thinking that's a red flag, too.

Rachelle doesn't seem to notice. "Are you sure Mom? I don't want you to be uncomfortable at home by yourself."

"Young lady, I've lived by myself for the past three years. I'm fine. I realize I've made a mess of things and dragged you into it, but I don't need a baby sitter, and you deserve to have a life." Jennifer smiles and her eyes light up as she turns her attention to me. "Now take my daughter on a date and make sure she enjoys herself."

"Yes ma'am," I say, high-fiving Rachelle's mom. I can't hide the excitement in my voice or my expression.

Glancing at Rachelle's computer screen, I take note of the time and realize I need to head back to Ugly Mug to get ready for the evening rush. Leaning down, I kiss Rachelle on the cheek and whisper, "I've got to get back to work."

She turns her head so her mouth is at my ear. "I'm done here at seven. I'll go to your apartment and order take out."

Jennifer notices the whispering between us and busies herself by getting a cup of coffee.

"You wouldn't rather go out somewhere?"

Rachelle shakes her head. "I'd rather just have you and some quiet time alone."

"Me too," I admit, kissing her cheek again. "I love you."

Rachelle doesn't just smile, she beams. "Love you, too."

I'm at my Jeep about to slide in the driver's side when Bing walks up.

"Gabe." He says my name in a tone that makes me think he has something on his mind.

"What's up, man?" I ask, glancing back toward Resolution. Rachelle waves from her desk.

"Are you paying Kristy's bills?" Bing's question lands

with the force of a right hook to the jaw.

"What makes you say that?" I'm kind of proud of myself for recovering quickly enough to answer him without stuttering.

"I know what she's doing is more than she could ordinarily do as a favor to someone." He shifts his weight and crosses his arms over his chest. "Like hiring private investigators to locate the asshole. Someone's footing the bill for that, and I know it's not her."

"And you think it's me?" I desperately don't want to lie to him, but there are reasons why I've kept my financial status a secret. "What's Kristy say?"

"She says from time to time generous people donate money so attorneys can do pro bono work."

"Well, there you go."

"Don't give me a load of shit, Jenkins. The only other person who cares as much about Rachelle and her mom as I do is you. Now Kristy didn't rat you out, and I have no idea where you're getting that kind of money, but I'm grateful… as long as you're not selling drugs or something else illegal."

Okay, I can't have Rachelle's brother wondering if I came by my money illegally. "It's not something I talk about. I've never wanted anyone to know because it's just not who I am, but it's all above board. It's my trust fund."

"Why would you not tell Rach?" he asks.

"Because I'm Gabe Jenkins, coffee shop manager." I don't add *potential* coffee shop owner. I've left Marshall and Janie a message that I'd like to sit down and talk with them about buying Ugly Mug, but so far we haven't been able to come up with a date for the meeting. "And that's all I've ever wanted to be. A normal guy who works hard, has friends, and does regular stuff. Money's never mattered to me."

"And that's admirable," he says. "But you need to be honest with her. This thing between you two is serious. All of us can see it. You can't have secrets if you love her."

"I do." He's right, and I know it. Just like I know my mom was right a couple of weeks ago. "I don't want her to think it's charity."

Bing nods. "She might for a minute, but if she's sure of your feelings for her, she'll know you're doing it because you love her. Because the two of you are a team."

"Don't say anything to her?" I phrase it as a question.

"I won't. It's your story to tell. But you gotta do it soon, Gabe."

I nod. Tonight. I'll tell her tonight about the money and about my dad. In my heart, I know it won't matter to her. She won't run screaming when she finds out that my father murdered my new stepmother right in front of me.

But a part of me dreads it just the same.

THE SIX CHINESE take-out boxes look great on my coffee table. Not because they're so cute or anything, but because there's twice as many as there used to be when I ordered Chinese just for myself. The significance of it hits me over the head.

I never want to order take-out for one again.

We're on our third *Doctor Who* episode, the remaining egg rolls and fortune cookies long forgotten, when my phone buzzes with a text.

I swipe to open it as Rachelle snuggles closer. I'm only half paying attention because on the TV, The Doctor is in the middle of his "Pandorica Opens" speech.

Beside me, Rachelle gasps, "Oh my gosh!"

I look down and a picture of Asher and Grace fills the screen. In the foreground, Grace's hand shows off the engagement ring Asher showed me earlier in the day.

I click to reply.

Told you she'd say yes!

"You knew?" Rachelle asks.

"Yeah, he told me when I was at the shop this afternoon. Showed me the ring, too."

She grabs my phone. "Let's send them a congratulatory picture."

We smash our faces together as Rachelle holds the phone far enough away to snap a selfie. The result is a picture of the two of us with ridiculous grins giving Asher and Grace two thumbs up.

After Rachelle hits send, I take the phone and set the picture as my wallpaper. She takes it back from me and opens the picture of Asher and Grace.

"They look so happy," she whispers.

"They are." I put my arm around her shoulder and pull her close.

"They kind of look like the opposite of us," she says. "He's got black hair and bronze skin, and she's fair skinned."

"I guess you're right." I run my fingers through her dark hair. "I love your dark hair and bronze skin."

"Do you think it's some kind of cosmic thing?" she asks. "Like the universe putting light and dark together? Kristy is blonde, and if Bing let his hair grow it would be dark brown."

"If you're supposed to be the *dark* in this scenario, I don't think there's anything cosmic to it." I lean over and kiss the top of her head. "I think if we're smart enough to recognize it and put the effort in, we wind up with exactly who we're meant to be with. If there's anything cosmic about it, I think it's more the way two lights are drawn to each other, like the way planets orbit stars."

She looks back at the picture of Asher and Grace and closes it, handing the phone back to me.

"Gabe?"

"Yeah."

"I'm really happy, too."

And just like that, all thoughts of telling her about my father and the money fly right out of my brain.

Chapter 38

GABE

IT'S TIME TO put this business with Sylvia to rest, once and for all.

I stare down at the article she sent me. I unearthed it from the junk drawer while searching for a rubber band. I pick up the short letter that accompanied the newspaper clipping and read her words again. Like everything Sylvia does, the letter was so very... civilized. There has never been any great love between Sylvia and me, but the last words I spoke to her were angry, and that's not how I want to leave things.

For my own sanity, I know I need to resolve things in a less antagonistic way.

Shoving the papers back into the junk drawer, I pull my phone from my pocket and dial.

She answers after the first ring.

"Gabriel." Her tone is the same as always. Proper and detached.

"Sylvia," I say. "I got your letter and the newspaper article."

"I hope this means you're considering a visit home,"

she replies. "I know your father would be thrilled to see you."

"Sylvia, stop." I keep my voice level and calm, but leave no room for her to argue. "I know you mean well. I know you're trying, in the only way you know how, to repair things. But you can't repair things between me and my father."

I hear her quick intake of breath. "If you'll just give him a chance to show you how much he's changed."

"I can't do that, Sylvia. Not after everything that's happened. I don't know if I'll ever be able to. And the more you try to force the issue, the more you're destroying any chance that I can ever feel anything for you other than contempt."

"Oh, Gabriel." Her voice breaks, surprising me. Displays of emotion have never been Sylvia's style. "I don't want you to hate me."

"I don't want that either," I say, amazed to realize I actually mean it. "There's been enough ugliness and heartache in our family. I need you to stop adding to it with the phone calls and the letters. If I'm ever going to consider seeing you again, it will have to be on my terms, and in my own time. You can't just pretend that we can go on as if nothing happened."

She's silent so long I begin to wonder if she's still there.

Finally, she speaks. "You witnessed things no human should ever witness, much less a young boy. For that, I'm sorry."

For a moment, I'm completely stunned. Though her words fall short of an admission of any wrong-doing on her part, it's the first time she's ever openly acknowledged that the things my father did were not right.

"Thank you," I whisper.

"I won't contact you again." I can hear the sadness and reluctance in her voice. "I'll hold out hope that one day you'll contact me. I realize that hope may be in vain, and I won't blame you."

"I wish you well, Sylvia. I mean that."

I end the call before she can reply and exhale in relief. I feel as though I've finally turned the page on an excruciating chapter of my life. I can't deny the sense of release coursing through me, but it's difficult to feel any sort of joy when I remember the sadness in Sylvia's voice.

Even still, there's a contentment in knowing I'm moving forward.

Grabbing my keys, I straighten my tie and head out the door. It's time to take the next step in my forward journey.

Chapter 39

RACHELE

THE NEXT SEVERAL days pass with my father and all my family drama blissfully absent from normal conversation. Everyone at Resolution and Ugly Mug is ecstatic about Asher and Grace's engagement. The discussion of wedding plans dominates the talk at both places.

Though they aren't planning to get married until next summer, Grace has already asked me to be a bridesmaid, along with her friend from high school, Sydney. So far, I've looked at pictures of seven different dresses and heard about twelve different color possibilities. It's cute, and I can't help but be happy for Grace.

Something's up with Gabe, too. This morning when I stopped in the shop for breakfast, he was practically giddy with excitement. When I asked him what was going on, he just smiled and said he didn't want to jinx it, but he hoped he'd have something big to share with me tonight.

So I'm surprised when Gabe calls Resolution just after my lunch break.

"Since when do you call the shop and not my cell?" I ask.

"Since I'm calling to see if Asher's got any time this afternoon," he says. I can almost hear the smile in his voice. "I know he's busier these days, so if he doesn't have time for ink, see if he's got a few minutes to look at my design. I've got a new idea, and I want his thoughts on it."

"His last appointment's at four, but let me check and see how long he's planning on hanging around after."

Putting Gabe on hold, I buzz Asher's room. He answers with a simple, "Yep."

"Gabe wants to know if you've got time this afternoon to do some ink," I begin. "If not, would you mind if he came in after your four o'clock to conference on the design. He's got something new to talk to you about."

"Grace has a study group for her board exams tonight, so I'm planning to stick around. Tell him to come on. I can probably go ahead and do it tonight."

I click the button to get Gabe back on the line. "Asher says come on in. He should be done by five or so, and he'll be here for a while after."

"Awesome," Gabe says. "I've been trying to nail down what I wanted to do with this star on my arm, and last night it just came to me. I also have some fantastic news to share with you, so I'm hoping you'll join me for dinner once Ash is done with me."

"Of course. But I wish you'd just tell me already. The suspense is killing me."

"No way," he chuckles. "I've got to set the stage for

news this big."

"Awful lot of big news around here these days. Asher and Grace, and now whatever you've got up your sleeve."

There's a pause, a beat of silence.

"Rach." Gabe's voice softens. "Don't worry. You don't need to be prepared with any sort of answer tonight. When I get ready to propose to you, I won't tell you I've got news. I'll surprise you with something special and romantic."

And… yeah. He totally just said *when*, not *if.*

Now I have to decide how to respond. Pretend that wasn't what I was thinking? Make some kind of silly remark? In the split second I have to make up my mind, I decide to just go with my heart.

"You melt my heart, Gabe," I whisper. "You know that?"

"I'm trying," he whispers back. "Every day."

"I love you."

"I love you, too, Rach. So much."

It's a good thing no one's in the lobby right now because I'm one big ball of mushy, gooey emotion.

"Will I see you when I come in for my appointment?" he asks.

"Yeah, I'll still be here."

"Good, I could use a kiss before I go under the needle."

✧   ✧   ✧

WHATEVER GABE'S GOT sketched on that piece of paper has Asher completely stoked.

"This is going to be epic," Asher says. "I love how it ties in with the ink you've already got."

"Why can't I see it?" I'm pouting on purpose. Gabe told me when he came in that I had to wait until it was a finished product. "So much secrecy tonight."

"I'll go get set up." Asher heads down the hall. "Come on back when you're ready."

"You can see it later tonight," Gabe says, grabbing me around the waist.

"And you'll tell me whatever big news has had you floating all day?" I wind my arms around his neck.

"Absolutely. It'll be like a double surprise."

And then he kisses me silly, like a man on top of the world. It takes my breath away. Every single time.

"Any time now!" Asher yells from his work-room.

Pulling apart, I take the arm he's about to have inked and place a kiss on the star that's already tattooed there. "Tell you what, I'll take care of getting dinner. You just meet me back at your place when you're done here."

"Sounds like a plan," he agrees.

I grab my purse and my keys, and then stick my head in the office door to let Bing know I'm cutting out.

"I'll walk you to your car before I let Asher loose on me." Gabe says, taking my hand. "Keep your eyes peeled and be safe. Harrison's working tonight, so if anything seems off, let him know."

And with that, I slide into my slick loaner car and take off, my biggest concern what to choose for a dinner full of surprises with the man I love.

Chapter 40

RACHELLE

OVER THE COURSE of our relationship, Gabe and I have done Chinese twice, homemade pizza, plenty of coffee and scones, not to mention the beautiful dinner we shared at The Brick. It's nice that we're both foodies who enjoy lots of different cuisines, but it makes it difficult to come up with something special for tonight.

Finally, I settle on Mediterranean. I have to Google the phone number for the hole-in-the-wall Greek joint that I've been to a few times. Fortunately, they do all kinds of take-out business, so they're able to take my order and have it ready within the hour.

Pushing my way into Gabe's apartment, I'm loaded down with shawarma, falafel, Greek salad, roasted red pepper hummus, and a six-pack of the expensive glass-bottle root beer that Gabe rarely buys for himself. Whatever he's got to share with me is a big deal to him, so I figure he deserves an upgrade on his soft drink.

Take out bags on the kitchen island, I take a look at the bottle of root beer, picking one up and testing the cap. Just what I thought. The caps aren't twist off. Surely

Gabe has a bottle opener in his kitchen. If not, I'll just run downstairs and ask Harrison.

I check the silverware drawer first. No luck. Next I open the cabinet where he keeps the glasses. Still no luck. Then, I remember the toothbrush he dug out of a junk drawer. Maybe that's where he keeps seldom-used gadgets.

Pulling open the drawer, I discover I was right. The bottle opener is right there in plain sight on top of a newspaper clipping and a handwritten letter. I know I'm being nosy, but the newspaper clipping grabs my curiosity. It must be important if he kept it. And he won't care if I take a look, right?

I look at the letter first. It's from his grandmother. Another attempt to get him to come back to Kansas City. He's told me how she tries all manner of emotional manipulation to get him to visit. Looks like this letter is more of the same.

> *Gabriel,*
>
> *I thought you might be interested in your father's recent accomplishment. While it may be difficult to believe, he is making great strides in atoning for his past behavior. I hope you'll take a moment to read, and perhaps consider a trip home in the near future.*
>
> *Sylvia Barlow Jenkins*

Except this time she included some sort of newspaper clipping about prisoners assisting in the clean up of storm-damaged buildings on the prison grounds. No names are mentioned, but there must be some connection. Reading over the letter again, one line jumps out at me. *He is making great strides in atoning for his past behavior.*

Gabe has never said anything about his father going to jail – not that it would be a shock for someone who physically abuses their spouse to wind up in prison, but it seems like something he would've mentioned.

I pull out my phone and open a browser. Quickly, I type words into the search bar.

Jenkins. Kansas City. Prison.

It doesn't take long to find a headline that fits.

Carlton Jenkins Could Face Life in Prison for Murder of Wife.

My body starts to tremble. I can't stop it, and I have to grab onto the kitchen island to steady myself. Scanning the first few paragraphs, I get the gist. Gabe's father stabbed and killed his new wife during a domestic dispute. Gabe was seventeen. He witnessed the murder.

The tears come without warning, spilling down my checks in rapid succession. Tears for the boy who experienced so much tragedy. Tears for the woman who lost her life. And tears that, for whatever reason, he couldn't share this with me.

And then it hits me like a ton of bricks. He didn't tell me. What does this mean for us? What does it mean that he couldn't, or wouldn't, tell me? We've shared so much these past months, or at least I thought we had. Looking back on it now, I see that I've done a whole lot of sharing. My childhood. My mom and her financial troubles. The fact that she's still legally married to my father. Gabe knows all of it. Once I decide to trust him… to let him in… I didn't hold back.

Part of me feels incredibly selfish for feeling hurt that he kept this part of his life from me. Clearly, he lived through hell during his childhood. But I lived through a similar hell, and I've opened my heart and my life to him completely. He knows every dark, unflattering thing about my family. I let him in because I thought we were building a partnership – one where we'd each share and lean on one another.

Why couldn't he do the same?

Wrapping my mind around it isn't going to happen in an instant.

Footsteps on the stairs yank me from my thoughts. Locking my phone screen, I drop it in my purse and sprint toward the bathroom.

Gabe's home, and I need a minute before I face him.

Chapter 41

GABE

SOMETHING IN MY apartment smells fantastic. I'm not one of those guys who wants a woman at home, cooking all the time, but I'm not going to lie – I love coming home, knowing Rachelle is here, and smelling dinner that she's prepared or ordered. Of course, it's not about the food at all. It's about the fact that she's here.

"Rach," I call as soon as I push the door open. "I'm home."

I hear water running in the bathroom and assume that's where she is. The black plastic taped across the inside of my forearm to protect my new ink is driving me nuts. To take my mind off it, I start nosing in the bags of food sitting on the island. I'm just about to pop open the lid of one of the styrofoam containers when I see the junk drawer open.

And then my stomach bottoms out when I see Sylvia's last letter and the newspaper article lying on the counter.

My heart pounds against my ribcage; my knees threaten to collapse, and there's no way to describe the amount of regret coursing through me. Why had I kept that article? Why hadn't I trashed it as soon as I opened it?

And the worst regret of all.

Why hadn't I told her the truth a long time ago?

She steps out of the bathroom. My heart sinks, my lungs refuse to work, and my blood runs cold.

She's been crying.

"Rachelle." My voice doesn't even sound like my own. It sounds like some desperate, pitiful attempt to convey how incredibly, unfathomably sorry I am for keeping the truth from her.

"Gabe," she says, her tone flat as she makes eye contact with me for a brief second, then dropping her eyes to the papers on the corner of the kitchen counter acknowledging that yes, in fact, she'd seen them. "I was looking for a bottle opener."

It's then I notice the carton of bottled root beer by the refrigerator. The kind I love but rarely buy for myself. She'd bought them for me. I feel like shit.

Nonchalantly, as if nothing at all is the matter, she walks toward the island in the center of the kitchen and reaches for her purse. I don't know how I know it, but deep down I'm certain that unless I say something, unless I initiate the inevitable confrontation, she's going to walk out of here without addressing it. And somehow I know that at this point that's the absolute worst thing that could happen.

"I'm so sorry," I whisper, touching her arm just before she grabs the strap of her purse. "Rachelle, you have no idea how sorry I am that I kept this from you."

"I'm not angry, Gabe." She pulls her arm away from me and takes a step back. I wish she'd be angry, though. I wish she'd yell, throw stuff, or slap me. Anything but this cold, detached demeanor she's got going right now.

"Why not?" I ask. It sounds stupid, questioning why she's not mad at me. I should be happy about that, but the lack of anger feels so unnatural that it scares the hell out of me.

"I'm disappointed." Her eyes finally meet mine again. "And hurt."

The words slice through me. I hate myself right now. I'd like to kick my own ass. Of all the things in the world I never wanted to do – like return to Kansas to live with Sylvia or try to reconcile with my father – disappointing Rachelle, hurting her, was at the very bottom of the list.

"Did you really think the truth about your father would scare me away?"

I shake my head. "I was humiliated. Ashamed. Ever since I left Kansas City, I've just wanted to leave it in the past."

"I get that," she says, nodding her head. "I do. More than most people. I totally understand not wanting to tell people all the ugly and unpleasant parts of your life. Because once you do, it's always attached to you. It changes the way people look at you, sometimes even how they treat you."

God, she really does understand. I knew she did, but

hearing the words come out of her mouth, expressing exactly what I've felt and why I've kept my past a secret. For a split second, I think maybe she can forgive me.

"But the thing is, Gabe," she goes on, "I trusted you not to do that. Not to look at me differently or treat me differently. I gave you all my worst secrets. I even felt bad for not telling you sooner. When you overheard me talking to Bing, I felt so guilty. So I swallowed my pride and trusted you with the truth, even though it was so far from pretty. Why you couldn't do the same."

My skin feels like it's been flayed open, jagged wounds gaping from the sting of her words. She's right. She's absolutely right.

"What can I do?" I ask. "Whatever you need, just say it."

"I need some time."

Except that. Anything but that. Logically, I understand. I know she needs time to process it all, to wrap her mind around it. But the thought of being apart from her, even for a little while, devastates me. My heart needs her in order to keep beating, or at least it seems that way. She's like oxygen, necessary and vital, and the thought of being separated from her feels like endless emptiness.

But I made this mess. I have no one to blame but myself, so if she needs time, I'll give it to her. I nod, letting her know I understand, and step toward her.

She grabs her purse and dodges me, heading around the other side of the island toward the door. With her hand on the knob, she stops.

"I'll be in touch," she says without turning around. "No matter what happens, I won't leave this hanging unresolved."

"Okay." My heart is splitting in two, and I know her assurance is more than I deserve.

She opens the door with a heavy sigh, her shoulders falling as if in defeat. I can't let her leave without saying something.

"I love you, Rachelle."

She looks over her shoulder. "I love you, too, Gabe. But right now, right at this moment, that's just not enough."

And then she's gone.

Chapter 42

RACHELLE

I'M OUT THE door and in the car in record time. Before, it's always been hard to leave Gabe's apartment. In some ways, it still is. It's difficult to leave knowing there's now this enormous distance between us. It's difficult to leave when I know I left a part of my heart in that apartment.

But it's also easier. Easier to leave than to stay and have to deal with the fact that he wasn't completely honest with me. Part of me realizes I'm running away, taking the easy way out, but I'm afraid that if I stay I'll say things I don't mean. Things I'd regret.

It only takes a few minutes to reach my duplex. Mom's car is already parked in the narrow driveway, so I pull in behind her. Mentally, I start making excuses for why I can't talk to her immediately, so I can escape to my room for a few minutes and get my emotions under control. I settle on claiming a desperate need to change clothes because I spilled something on myself, but it turns out my excuse isn't necessary.

Because Mom's sitting at the table having coffee and

dessert of some kind with Mr. Grainger.

I can tell I've surprised them when Mom quickly pipes up. "Rachelle. I thought you were having dinner at Gabe's?"

"Last minute change of plans," I say. "You two enjoy your dessert. I'm just going to go change clothes."

I can't get into my bedroom fast enough. Not that the thought of my mom with Mr. Grainger is that bad – it's actually not bad at all. He's a nice man, and I'd be fine if the two of them connected, but Mom's mired in a whole heap of shit right now, and I hardly think it's fair to drag poor Mr. Grainger into all the bankruptcy and divorce drama.

Not to mention it's just plain awkward to walk in on your mom on a semi-date with your landlord.

I don't know if Mom could tell something was wrong when I came in, or if she and Mr. Grainger just decided to cut their evening short because I came home early, but I can hear the two of them saying their good-byes. I shrug out of my work clothes and throw on a pair of ratty gray yoga pants and an oversized Resolution tee shirt that hangs off one shoulder. I pile my hair into a messy bun on top of my head and root around in the bottom of my closet until I find my favorite pair of leather flip-flops.

I'm chewing my thumbnail and pacing my room when I hear the front door shut.

"You may as well come out and tell me what's got you so upset," Mom calls.

I should've known I couldn't hide it from her.

I open my bedroom door with reluctance, and Mom is standing there. It doesn't matter that I've been miffed at her over the non-divorce and the credit card debt or that I pride myself on making my own way and being independent. At this moment, I just want my mom.

I promptly erupt into tears and fling myself into her arms.

Somehow, we make it to the couch, and between the tears and sobs, I tell her everything. I tell her what I know about Gabe's childhood, what he and his mother endured. I tell her how in love with him I am. And I tell her what he kept from me, despite the fact that he knew everything about me.

"What an awful, awful thing for a boy to have to go through," Mom says. "To see his father abuse his mother and then to witness the murder of his stepmother."

I can't do anything but nod. And sniffle.

"And Gabe has turned into such a sweet and gentle man," Mom says. "It's almost like he refused to let the ugliness of his childhood touch him, and he turned into the exact opposite kind of man his father is."

Leave it to my mom to put it so simply, yet so beautifully.

The crying commences again because I realize that I only took a small moment to consider what Gabe had endured, to be sad for all he'd seen and experienced as a child. I only spent a few seconds to feel heartbreak for him before I started feeling sorry for myself. Before I started questioning his love and his loyalty, thinking the fact that he'd kept it from me had to mean something huge and significant.

When the truth is, Gabe just doesn't let the ugliness touch him anymore. My mom is right. He took something awful and built something beautiful, and I honestly cannot fault him for being reluctant to let the ugliness out into the light.

I get up and walk to the kitchen for the box of tissues I know is on the counter. When I return to the sofa, Mom is reading something on her phone. Her expression is intent, followed by horrified.

"He testified against his father at the trial," she says. Apparently, she looked up the incident online just like I did.

I sink onto the couch, trying without success to imagine how conflicted he must've felt.

"The father refused a plea deal, so the case went to trial. Gabe was the state's primary witness because he saw it happen."

"Oh Gabe," I sigh, to no one but myself.

My cell rings, and Bing's name flashes on the screen. "Hello."

"Gabe's going nuts trying to find you," he says, launching into it without so much as a greeting. "He says the two of you had an argument and you left."

"I'm home with Mom," I say. "And I feel terrible about the argument."

"He filled me in." Bing's voice is short. "On everything. You need to know something."

"What?" I ask, pushing up from the couch and walking toward my bedroom. Something tells me I need a little privacy for this.

"I promised I wouldn't tell you because it was Gabe's story to tell, but given what's happened today, I think you need to hear it."

"You're scaring me, Bing."

"Gabe's family has a lot of money. He has a trust fund with a shit ton of money in it. Money he hadn't touched since the moment it became his when he turned twenty-one." He pauses, and I hold my breath. "Until now."

A sinking feeling punches me in the gut. "Why now?"

"He's been paying Kristy's bills. She's doing what she can for nothing, but the private investigators and some of the other things… he paid for those. He didn't want you to know."

Sweet, generous Gabe. My heart swells with love and breaks at the same time. "Why wouldn't he tell me?"

"My guess is he was ashamed of the money, didn't want it because it was connected to his father, and he didn't want you think it was pity or charity."

"I wouldn't have thought that," I argue.

"Really?" he asks. "Because I think that might've been your initial reaction."

I'm silent, so Bing goes on.

"You've worked hard to build a life for yourself. I

understand that because I've walked that road, too. Sometimes it's hard to accept help, even from people who love us. And that's why Gabe did this. Not because he thought you couldn't handle it, but because he loves you, and he wants to make your life better. Even if you never knew he did it."

"I'm so stupid." I pace back and forth between the door and my bed. "I can't believe I walked out on him the way I did. He told me he loved me, and I told him right now that wasn't enough."

"It'll be okay," Bing says. "Just talk to him. He's crazy worried about you."

"I'll call him right now. If you talk to him before I do, tell him –"

A huge crashing noise followed by a scream from the living room send me barreling out of my room. I skid to a stop at the end of the hallway. My mom is cowering against the wall, the remnants of a table lamp scattered around her. In the open doorway stands my dad, a pistol dangling from his right hand.

I drop my hand to my side, hoping he won't notice the cell phone, but naturally he does.

"Just toss that phone away, girl." His voice is slurred, but he still manages a nasty sneer. "Don't get any big ideas about calling the cops on me again."

"Okay, Dad," I say, loud enough for Bing to hear if he's still on the line. Looking over my shoulder, I lob the phone as easy as I can, hoping that when it lands Bing will still be able to hear. "Don't hurt us. Just tell us what you want."

"I want you to call off the damn police!" he yells. "They keep nosing around, asking people where to find me. I can't go anywhere anymore!"

I'm pretty sure I don't want to know what kind of places my dad frequents, since my guess is they all deal with alcohol, drugs, and no telling what else.

"We didn't call the cops," I say, forcing my voice to stay calm when inside I want to scream and rage at him. "We called a lawyer."

"What's the difference?" he shouts, swinging the gun around as he gestures erratically with his hands. "They're all dirty crooks anyway."

Mom inches along the wall, closer to me, until finally she's right beside me. It's all too familiar. We wrap our arms around each other, the hallway behind us so we at least have a place to run if it becomes necessary.

"The credit cards." Mom's voice is soft. I can feel her trembling next to me. "We owed so much money that I couldn't keep up with the payments. I called an attorney to help me figure out how to manage it."

I don't fail to notice her use of the pronoun *we*. She's aligning herself with him, making it seem like a shared problem rather than a screw-up he created on his own.

"If the police are looking for you, Dad, it's not because of us." I can't see out the front door because he's blocking it, but I can hear the sounds of traffic passing by. Couldn't just one of them notice the crazed, drunk man and call 911?

"You expect me to believe that shit?" He staggers closer, and Mom and I back up a step into the hall. "You expect me to believe anything that comes out of your mouth after your piece of shit man-whore assaulted me?"

It's on the tip of my tongue to tell him *he* was the one guilty of assault and all Gabe did was defend me. And I'd like to vehemently defend Gabe against the man-whore insult, but antagonizing him while he's armed would be monumentally unwise. Not to mention it would fall on drunken, deaf ears anyway.

"Okay, okay." In the tiny bit of space between my dad and the doorjamb, something outside catches my eye. It's movement from near the road. Not a car. It must be a person. Maybe someone out for a walk. If I could just make enough noise to get their attention... but then I see the gun hanging in his hand and think better of it. "If you want us to call the lawyer and have her stop the cops from looking for you, you're going to have to let me get my phone."

"Move slow," he says and then waves the gun in Mom's direction. "And she stays right there."

I squeeze Mom and start backing down the hall, keeping my eyes glued to him. He steps away from the door so he can keep watch on me as I move backwards.

Gabe steps into the open doorway, followed by Mr. Grainger. My breath catches, but I don't outwardly react. Gabe's wearing a dark, navy zip-up sweatshirt, the hood pulled up and over, almost reaching his eyes. Mr. Grainger's eyes are on Mom, his finger raised to his lips, a reminder to keep silent. My heart is pounding against my chest, as I bend down to grasp my phone. Bing's call has disconnected, which is most likely the reason Gabe and Mr. Grainger are here.

Before I can stand back up, I see Gabe gesture for me to stay down. Mom is inching along the living room wall toward the kitchen. Dad's at the entrance to the hall now, his eyes trained on me, unaware that Mom has moved.

Still crouched in the hallway next to my bedroom door, I watch as Mr. Grainger slips in the front door and motions Mom toward him. Gabe moves inside as well, stepping almost directly behind my dad.

"Hurry up, you bitch," Dad yells. "Pick up the phone, and make the call!"

I nod and grasp the phone, pulling it up and pretending to dial without standing up. His arm hangs limp at his side, the gun pointing toward the floor. Behind him, Gabe tilts his head and motions toward my bedroom door and at the same time he reaches for Dad's hand.

He's going to try and disarm him. If I weren't already on the floor, my knees would've collapsed and landed me here anyway. Fear courses through me, a sheen of sweat breaking out across my skin. My dad is drunk. He has a gun. Gabe is unarmed. The possibilities are frightening.

As Gabe's hand closes around my dad's wrist, I drop to the floor and roll into my bedroom.

The sound of the gun is deafening inside my small

duplex. I hear my mom scream, followed by a heavy thud as someone falls.

I'm frozen on the floor of my bedroom, terrified of going out there to see what happened. The gun went off. Mom screamed. Someone fell. I can't hear anything now because my pulse is pounding so hard in my ears. My chest is rising and falling with alarming speed. I can't hyperventilate right now. I have to call the police.

Bending at the waist, I put my head near my knees and try to slow my breathing. I force myself to remember that Gabe is out there, and whatever happened, he needs me. It only takes a few seconds for my breaths to slow.

I'm just about to hit the button to call when I hear Gabe's voice.

"Rachelle!" He doesn't sound hurt. He sounds strong. And whole.

Pushing to my feet, I stumble into the hallway. Quickly, I survey the situation. There's a hole in my floor from the gunshot. My dad is lying face down beside it, struggling as Gabe sits on top of him. The gun is behind them, out of Dad's reach. Mom is in Mr. Grainger's arms, weeping softly as he comforts her.

I don't know what to do. I want to run to Gabe and jump into his arms, but he's restraining my dad, so that's out of the question. I want to apologize and tell him how much I love him. I want to scream at my dad for all the hurt he's caused us. But I do none of those things.

Instead, I just stand there and cry.

Suddenly, Bing is in the room followed by two police

officers. I'd been so caught up in everything I hadn't even heard them approach. It takes less than a split second for the officers to take over with my dad, and then, Gabe is on his feet coming toward me.

And then I'm in his arms. I plaster my face against his chest and he buries his in my neck. We stand like that for a long time, holding each other and breathing together, assuring ourselves over and over again that we are safe and unharmed. I hear the police handcuff my father. They're talking to Mom and Mr. Grainger, too, and I know Gabe and I are going to have to speak with them as well. Before we do, there are things I have to say to Gabe.

"I'm so sorry," I whisper, leaning up just enough to look at him. "So sorry."

He shakes his head. "Don't apologize. I should've told you."

"You would've. In your own time. I know that now. I know you wouldn't have kept it from me forever. I was so wrong to be so harsh, to walk out on you like that. It was wrong, and I'm sorry."

"It doesn't even matter anymore," he says, unwrapping his arms from around me and framing my face in his hands. "You're here, and you're safe. That's all that matters."

"I love you so much, Gabe. You have to know that. Nothing can change that."

Our lips crash together, like we're the only two people in the room. The intensity isn't born out of passion, but rather relief and gratitude. When we pull apart, we make our way into the living room, arms still around one another, to deal with whatever needs to be done to wrap up this unpleasantness.

My dad is detained in the backseat of the police car, and rather than taking statements from us now, the officers suggest we each come to the station tomorrow morning. No one argues. We're all too tired and frazzled to do much good tonight.

"I'll call someone first thing in the morning to come repair the floor," Mr. Grainger says.

"If you need us to help pay for the repairs," I begin, but Mr. Grainger stops me.

"I have insurance, of course," he says. "Don't worry about the bill."

"We'll get a hotel room for the time being." I look at Mom. "We'll pack what we need and stay there until everything's settled."

"No." Gabe's voice comes out of nowhere. "You two can stay with me. The two of you can have the queen-sized, and I'll take the couch." His tone leaves no room for argument. "Mr. Grainger, please let me help you expedite the repair process, even if it costs more. I want things back to normal for Rachelle and Jennifer as quickly as possible."

"Gabe, you don't have to do that." Of course, I put up an argument despite the fact that I know he won't let me. "You can't want to sleep on the couch again."

"I want you under my roof tonight," he replies. His

eyes soften as he looks at me. "If you're not, I may lose my mind."

"Let him take care you." This coming from Bing.

I look at Mom, who nods.

"Well, alright then. I guess that's that."

Chapter 43

GABE

IT'S PAST TEN in the morning, and Rachelle's still asleep. After what she went through last night, I don't fault her. Bing told her not to even think about coming in to work today, and Jennifer arranged to take the day off as well, but that didn't stop her from being up at the crack of dawn.

Apparently, she and Mr. Grainger had made plans to meet for breakfast before heading to the police station to give their statements. The two of them seemed quite smitten with each other, and I'm glad. She deserves to be happy, and it'll give Rachelle a huge measure of comfort to know her mom is with someone as kind and caring as Mr. Grainger.

When Jennifer left, I went downstairs to check on things, and while I was down there, I grabbed two dirty chai lattes and a bag full of scones. Now, I'm slipping back into the still quiet-apartment, breakfast in hand.

Setting the breakfast on the coffee table, I round the corner into my bedroom and see Rachelle on the far side of the bed, her dark hair spread out on my pillow and her face peaceful and relaxed. My breath catches, and a lump forms in my throat. She's so beautiful, and she looks so right in my bed.

Slowly, I lower onto the bed until I'm sitting beside her. She stirs, just a bit, and I reach up to smooth a few loose hairs away from her face. She turns into my touch, nuzzling her cheek against my palm, the movement so instinctive and natural that she does it despite still being half asleep.

"Good morning, babe," I whisper, mesmerized by the sight of her eyelids fluttering open.

"Hi," she says with a lazy smile. For a second, she takes in her surroundings, then asks, "Where's Mom?"

"She and Mr. Grainger made plans for a breakfast date before going to the police station."

She giggles, and my heart does this strange twisting and expanding in my chest. "I had no idea about the two of them until last night when I walked in they were having coffee and dessert. I could tell they weren't expecting me."

"I think it's sweet," I say.

Rachelle nods. "He's always seemed a bit lonely, and heaven knows, my mom's had her share of bad luck with men. I hope it works out for them."

"Well, since your mom and Mr. Grainger had a breakfast engagement, I thought it only fair that you did, too." I gesture toward the living room. "Dirty chai and scones await you, my lady."

"I'm going to make use of my toothbrush first." She

reaches up to feel her hair. "And maybe your hairbrush, too."

"Like I told you, you're welcome to anything in there." I lean over and kiss her forehead. "I'll be in the living room waiting."

Rachelle emerges a few moments later, her hair brushed smooth and pulled into a knot on top of her head. Her face, free of any trace of make-up, is flushed from what must've been a splash of warm water. Still in the yoga pants and big tee shirt from the night before, she looks just as gorgeous as ever.

I meet her halfway and wrap my arms around her, breathing in the soft scent of her, baking in the warmth radiating from her. Thoughts of what could've happened last night if I hadn't gotten to her in time creep into the edges of my mind, but I push them away. She safe, and she's here.

"Breakfast is served," I say with a wink, taking her hand and leading her to the sofa.

Coffee and scones are easy for us. They're familiar and comforting, and, as strange as it seems, a part of the fibers of our history together. I let that comfort simmer around us and enjoy that sense of familiarity, putting off the conversation about our argument that I know we need to have.

I know we said our *I'm Sorries* last night, but the fact is, we hurt each other. Not intentionally, but the hurt happened nonetheless, and no way do I want any shred of that hurt hanging around, threatening to flare back up the moment we argue again. And I know we'll argue again. It's part of being in a relationship, part of loving someone. What I want to be certain of is that we know how to put each other first and work through things together.

Rachelle pops the last bite of scone in her mouth and closes her eyes, savoring the lemon poppy seed flavor. I suppose now is as good a time as any.

"I should've told you," I whisper. "I should've trusted you."

She takes a deep breath before opening her eyes. "I know it wasn't because you don't trust me. I should never have accused you of that."

"Still, it was wrong of me to keep it from you for so long."

She turns toward me, pulling her legs up to sit cross-legged on the couch. "I wish you'd told me yourself so I didn't have feel the shock of finding out the way I did. But I should've waited for you, asked you for the truth, rather than looking online and just assuming you hid it from me for the wrong reasons."

"I wasn't hiding it from you." I reach for her hands, enveloping them in my own. "I was hiding it from everyone. I thought that if I just didn't talk about it, it would be like it never happened. This life, here in Flagstaff, with my mom, with you and all our friends, it's the kind of life I always dreamed about. The kind of life I thought I'd never have. And now that I'm living it, I just didn't want any part of my father to touch it."

"He can't touch what you've built here." She tilts her head, trapping my gaze with hers. "He can't touch what we've built together."

"Does this mean you forgive me?" I ask, a small grin on my face.

"Only if you forgive me," she replies.

"How about we agree to forgive each other?"

She nods, squeezing my hands. "Gabe, what you went through." She stops, closes her eyes, and takes a deep breath. "I know what it's like to watch your father hurt your mother. It's terrible. It messes with your faith in humanity, in your belief in the goodness that most people possess. But what you witnessed with your stepmother?" Her voice trembles, then breaks. "That's another level of depravity that I can't even comprehend. And then for you to have to testify against your own father? Gabe, when I look at you now, knowing who you are and what you've become, I'm so amazed, and so proud. There is *nothing* of your father in you. You are the best man I've ever known."

Something inside me shifts with her words, like a dam breaking, the water rushing outward and affirming something deep in my heart. So many thoughts jumble inside my head, that it's impossible to form a sentence. All I know is that hearing her say that I'm the best man she's ever known makes me incredibly, deliriously happy.

I take her face between my palms and lower my lips to hers. There's no preamble, no subtlety, just a wild clashing of mouths. She grips handfuls of my sweatshirt and pulls me closer. I press my lips along her jaw, until I get to her ear, and whisper, "Being a man good enough for you is my greatest accomplishment."

"Will you tell me about it?" she asks, her voice soft, still dreamy from our kiss. I know she means my father and the death of my stepmother. I'm finished keeping even the most minute detail from her. If she wants to hear it, I'm going to share it.

"Ginger, my stepmother, wasn't a bad person," I start. "I never really got to know her very well because I kept myself otherwise occupied, and my father didn't care what I thought anyway. But Ginger was nice. She was just young and foolish, and she fell for everything he told her. Once they were married, it didn't take her long to figure out the kind of man he really was. I felt sorry for her, but she wasn't going to stick around and let him treat her like garbage. She was leaving. That's what they argued about that day. I came home in the middle of it, and instead of going straight upstairs to my room, I hung around in the kitchen while they argued in the living room. I was kind of proud of her for sticking up for herself."

I close my eyes, allowing myself to call up memories I've kept buried for years. It's not hard. The images are burned into my brain. "I heard a crash, and I knew he'd thrown something at her, so I walked to the doorway. She was lying on the floor, shards of glass from a vase all around her. He walked over, knelt down, picked up one of the larger shards…"

"You don't have to go on." Rachelle's words stop me, sparing me the worst of it.

"You know, the worst part of it, other than the fact that Ginger died, was that I wasn't even surprised. I watched my own father kill someone, and I wasn't the least bit shocked. I'd known for a long time he was capable of it. That's why I made sure Mom left when she did."

"But then you had to testify against him."

"That wasn't pleasant, but it wasn't hard either. I was almost glad for the chance to get up on that stand and tell the whole world what kind of bastard my father truly was. He was furious with me, but I didn't care. I answered some questions about what I'd seen him do to my mom, I guess to establish a pattern of violent behavior. And, of course, I testified about what I'd seen the day he killed Ginger. It was cathartic, in a way, to get it all out in the open, to say it for everyone to hear, to have my words part of a public record that detailed the criminal he was. In a way, it freed me of him, I guess, and maybe that's why I've been able to just move on with my life and make something new."

"Gabe, I need to thank you." She scoots closer and lowers her voice. "For everything with Kristy. Using your money to help my mom was extremely kind and generous."

I shake my head. "You don't have to thank me. I'd been waiting for a reason to use that money. It never felt right just to spend it on material things. I hated the idea of having some kind of luxury that was paid for with his money. I always wanted to use it for something good." I reach up and trace the outline of her jaw. "And you're the best thing that's ever happened to me, so what better way to spend it."

Rachelle's eyes are wet with tears that spill over. She smiles through them, and places her hand against my cheek. "When I told you yesterday that love wasn't enough, I was wrong. Love, when it's true and pure, is *everything*. And I love you, Gabe Jenkins, with everything in me, and because of that, nothing will tear us apart."

A soft press of lips later, she goes on. "Now, will you please show me that new tattoo? I'm dying to see what it is."

"In a minute. But I want to tell you something first," I say. "I'm going to buy Ugly Mug."

Chapter 44

GABE

RACHELLE'S EYES GO wide. "When did this happen?"

"Marshall and Janie told me a few weeks ago that they were going to sell." I explain. "I was worried whoever bought the place would want to hire their own manager. Mom convinced me I should use the money from my trust fund to buy the place. We sat down yesterday and discussed the details. Paperwork and all that will happen really soon."

"Gabe, that's fantastic!" She throws her arms around me and squeezes tight. "You'll be a perfect business owner!"

"I don't know about perfect, but I guess I know enough about this place to not screw up too badly."

She unwraps herself from me and settles back on the couch. "What about the place in Phoenix?"

"Owning two, in two different cities, would be more than I need to tackle right off the bat. They've got an interested buyer in Phoenix, so hopefully that works out for them. And if I decide I want to expand, I'd rather do it here in Flagstaff."

"I'm so proud of you." Her words and the smile on her face mean more to me that I could ever explain.

I reach up and unzip my sweatshirt, pulling one sleeve off and then the next, careful to keep my arm turned to where Rachelle doesn't see the tattoo. The skin around it is still a bit red, but when I smeared the ointment on it earlier this morning, it had lessened enough that the design really popped.

"What?" she asks with a chuckle. "Is it a naked girl or something? Is that why you don't want to show me?"

"Of course not," I say, laughter lacing my voice.

But when I lay my arm down across her thigh, the new tattoo staring her in the face, I'm quiet and serious. I hope she remembers… and understands.

For a long moment she just stares, but then I hear her breath hitch and her hand comes up to cover her mouth.

"Oh Gabe!"

"You remember?"

She nods, her eyes still glued to the snapshot of a galaxy on my arm.

What had been a just common star tattoo that I chose without much thought, simply to give Asher an opportunity to practice, has been transformed into a lifelike image of a white giant. The rays of light shoot out in streaks of brilliant energy. A planet looms close, unwavering in its orbit around its source of light. Several small stars can be seen in the distance, bearing witness to the powerful connection between the two beings.

"Two lights are drawn to each other," she whispers. When she looks up, her eyes are wet with unshed tears.

"You're my light, Rach, and I'm forever in your orbit."

Epilogue

Six weeks later...

RACHELLE

U GLY MUG IS full of all my favorite people tonight, gathered together to celebrate Asher and Grace's engagement. Gabe owns the shop, and he was happy to close up early on a Tuesday evening so we could honor our friends and their upcoming marriage.

The espresso machine is working constantly, with Harrison at the helm, and Asher's mom, Stella, made the most amazingly delicious cupcakes and cookies. It's a perfect party, not just because of the coffee and desserts, but also because of the sense of happiness that hangs in the air like a sweet smelling perfume.

"I think your brother is in love." Gabe steps close behind me, sliding his arms around my waist and leaning down to whisper in my ear. "It looks good on him."

It's true. Bing looks happy and completely smitten as he sits across a small table from Kristy. In his lap Kristy's son, Ezra, is sipping hot chocolate, leaving him with a whipped cream mustache. The gleam in Bing's eyes tells me that he's fallen in love with not only Kristy, but Ezra as well. Some would look at Bing and think he'd never make a good family man, but I know different. His capacity to love is enormous, and it appears Kristy and Ezra are the lucky recipients.

"I'm so happy for him," I say, turning enough that I can press a kiss to Gabe's cheek. "He's such a good man."

"He is," Gabe agrees. "And Kristy and her boy are lucky to have him."

That Gabe thinks so highly of my brother means so much to me.

"Your mom and Mr. Grainger are looking chummier than usual."

I can't help but laugh. "Yes. I think she finally picked a winner."

"She deserves it." Gabe tightens his arms around me. "It's been a long time coming for her."

Gabe's mom, Andrea, sits a table with Mom and Mr. Grainger, the three of them carrying on like friends who've known each other for a lifetime. Perhaps my mom has finally found her place in the world. The thought makes me smile.

"Who's the girl with Caleb?" I ask. My eyes wander over to the counter where Caleb, his date, and Shane are huddled together.

"Her name's Felicity," Gabe answers. "He hasn't elaborated on where he met her. Apparently, they've been seeing each other for a couple of months."

"Shane looks lonely," I say with a sigh. Shane has

always been a bit of a free spirit – not a player necessarily, but certainly not someone who wanted to be tied down for any length of time. But now, for the first time since I've known Shane, it seems like maybe he wishes he had someone by his side.

"Maybe he's finally ready to settle a bit," Gabe suggests. "Find a nice girl he can spend time with and get to know."

Just then, Asher's father, Dave Howell, claps loudly to get everyone's attention. On one side is his new wife, Amelia, and on the other, Asher's mom, Stella.

"I just want to take a moment to let you all know how grateful we are for all of you," he begins. "When your first child leaves home to make his way in the world, it's hard to let go. Stella and I worried, but after getting to know all of you, I can see we worried needlessly. Thank you for becoming family to him, and for always loving him and Grace."

Grace's mom, Paula, is next. "We feel the same way," she says, taking her husband's hand. "You all have made this transition so much easier, knowing Grace is among such good friends. We're so happy that she and Asher will begin their married life with all of you alongside them."

"When's the date?" Shane shouts, interrupting the melancholy of the moment.

All eyes turn toward Asher and Grace. This is the announcement everyone's been waiting for.

"May twentieth," Asher says, and applause sounds

from all around the room.

"Looks like we'll have a wedding to attend this spring." I lean back against Gabe's chest, enjoying the feeling of being wrapped in his embrace.

"Looks like," he says. "Will you be my date?"

Laughing, I elbow him gently in the ribs.

The festivities carry on for a while before people start leaving. Bing and Kristy are the first to go. It's a school night for Ezra and it's already past his bedtime. An hour or so later, Asher and Grace's parents all head out to make the drive back to Greyson. Mom and Mr. Grainger, along with Andrea, make their exit around eleven. Caleb and Felicity, along with Shane and Asher and Grace, are the last to go, hanging around until nearly midnight to help to get the place cleaned up.

And then it's just Gabe and me.

Gabe locks the front door and flips the main light off, the room now illuminated by the indirect light over the counter that always stays on.

"I should head home, too," I say. "I have payroll to tackle in the morning."

Gabe nods, coming over to take my hand. We walk toward the back of the shop, and stop by the door that opens to the staircase leading up to his apartment. He turns to face me, his palm resting against my cheek as his thumb traces circles under my eye.

"I'm tired of saying goodbye to you at the end of every night," he whispers.

"Gabe," I say, my voice barely more than breath. "I

GABE'S SECRET

know we haven't talked about the spending the night issue. You've been so sweet about it all, and I …"

He interrupts. "That's not what I'm talking about. I mean, it sort of is, but not in the way you think. I'm not trying to push you."

Stepping closer, he takes both my hands. I don't say anything. I just keep my gaze fixed on his.

"I want you with me. All the time." He places a kiss on my forehead and leans back to look at me again. "In my apartment. My bed. I want more than just your toothbrush in my bathroom."

I smile, loving his words but still unsure where he's going.

"This is mine," he says, looking around the shop. "I can't believe it, but it is. I want to share it with you. I don't want to do anything without you, ever. You're it for me, Rach."

Letting go of my left hand, he reaches in his pocket. My heart seems to stop, then begin again with a thunderous rhythm in my chest. I don't remember holding my breath, but when he pulls out a dark purple velvet ring box, whatever air was in my lungs comes rushing out.

"Marry me, Rachelle. I love you, and I'll be devoted to you as long as I live. Share this life with me." He flips the lid of the box open, revealing a simple white gold band with a square cut diamond. "Will you be my wife?"

I'm so overwhelmed by his words I can do nothing but nod. Looking up from the ring to his face, the

255

emotion swimming across his expression is nearly my undoing. His eyes are wet with tears, as I'm sure mine are. With shaking hands, he takes the ring from the box and slides it on my finger.

Gabe tosses the ring box on the nearest table, grabs my face, and pulls me forward in a searing kiss. This kiss is different than all the others we've shared before. It's full of promise... full of possibility... full of the brightness of our future.

Grinning like idiots, we pull apart and just stare at one another.

"Are you okay with a long engagement?" I ask.

His face pales slightly as he calculates his answer. "If that's what you want."

I can't help the mischievous laugh that bubbles up from inside me as I shake my head and say, "It's not."

Gabe throws his head back and laughs, then picks me up and swings me around in a circle.

"Thank God." He puts my feet on the floor but doesn't let go. "The sooner the better."

"Guess we're planning another engagement party." I push up to my tiptoes so I can press my lips against his. "Or we just skip it altogether and throw a wedding instead."

"Are you serious?" he asks.

"I am." I put my hand against his chest, feeling the strength of his heartbeat beneath my palm. "Let's talk dates."

Gabe's smile is brilliant, blinding even. "I love you so

much."

"I love you, too." I reach around and slap his backside playfully. "Now let's figure out when we're going to turn me into Mrs. Jenkins."

"I love the sound of that," he says, pulling me to him again. Leaning down, he presses his lips against my forehead. "I'll make you happy, Rachelle. I'll never stop."

"Same goes, Gabe. For the rest of my life."

And there, in the dim lights of Ugly Mug, our life together begins.

THE END

A NOTE FROM AMY DURHAM...

If you enjoyed this book, please consider leaving a review at your place of purchase and/or any other online review site you frequent. Customer reviews are one of the best ways to show an author you enjoyed his or her work and can be invaluable for other readers as they browse for reading material. This author reads all reviews and greatly appreciates each one.

About the Author

After spending every work day with classrooms full of tweens and teens, then going home to three boys of her own, two of whom fall into the tween/teen category, you'd think that Amy Durham might like to leave the world of teenagers and young adults behind.

Not so! Instead, she spends her spare moments – which sometimes consist of waiting twenty minutes for her kiddos to get out of band practice – with her laptop and a multitude of teenage characters trying to navigate their way through the twisted, difficult road of adolescence.

You might ask… "Why Young/New Adult Fiction"? Well, because it's what she knows. As a teacher and a parent, Amy is around teens on an almost constant basis. And while it's true they can be – ahem – challenging, they are also full of life, vision, and dreams. And that's a really cool place to be.

Young Adult and New Adult Fiction allows young readers the opportunity to find hope for the situations they find themselves in, find determination to keep on going, and courage to pursue their dreams. It also allows adult readers the chance to revisit the exuberance of youth, remember the joy and poignancy of first love, and recall how it felt to dream with abandon.

Amy Durham is a wife and mother, an author, a teacher, an avid reader, and a musician. If she weren't writing books, she'd be a celebrity chef!

Contact Amy online at:
www.amydurham.com
amybdurham@gmail.com
facebook.com/AuthorAmyDurham
Twitter: twitter.com/Amy_Durham
Instagram: @AuthorAmyDurham